Sarazanmai

NOVEL

1

D0095749

WRITTEN BY

Kunihiko Ikuhara
Teruko Utsumi

Seven Seas Entertainment

SARAZANMAI NOVEL VOLUME 1
by Ikuhara Kunihiko / Utsumi Teruko / miggy

Original Japanese edition published in 2019 by
GENTOSHA COMICS Inc.
English translation rights arranged worldwide with
GENTOSHA COMICS Inc. through Digital Catapult Inc., Tokyo.

Seven Seas press and purchase enquiries can be sent to
Marketing Manager Lianne Sentar at press@gomanga.com.
Information regarding the distribution and purchase of
digital editions is available from Digital Manager CK Russell
at digital@gomanga.com.

Seven Seas and the Seven Seas logo are trademarks of
Seven Seas Entertainment. All rights reserved.

Follow Seven Seas Entertainment online at
sevenseasentertainment.com.

TRANSLATION: Alyssa Orton-Niioka
ADAPTATION: Nino Cipri
COVER DESIGN: Nicky Lim
INTERIOR LAYOUT & DESIGN: Clay Gardner
PROOFREADER: Kelly Lorraine Andrews, Kat Adler
LIGHT NOVEL EDITOR: Nibedita Sen
PREPRESS TECHNICIAN: Rhiannon Rasmussen-Silverstein
PRODUCTION MANAGER: Lissa Pattillo
MANAGING EDITOR: Julie Davis
ASSOCIATE PUBLISHER: Adam Arnold
PUBLISHER: Jason DeAngelis

ISBN: 978-1-64505-728-4
Printed in Canada
First Printing: September 2020
10 9 8 7 6 5 4 3 2 1

TABLE OF CONTENTS

Three Children

YOU AND I were connected since that freezing cold night when peach-colored petals danced through the air, through those evenings after school as the dazzling emerald foliage grew thick.

We've come so very far, but I can't help but wonder if you've forgotten me.

There are children in this town that carry secrets. They live with hearts full of loneliness, lying to themselves, stealing from others. But is that so wrong? A secret stays a secret only so long as it's not revealed. They've buried those feelings so deep inside their hearts, God himself couldn't touch them.

I remember the hand I batted away, and that trembling gaze. I remember the darkness illuminated by a flash of light, a body cold to the touch. I remember you, smiling innocently, and the feel of your lips. There isn't a single day that I don't remember.

I can't connect with you, but my wishes—they're all for you.

Sarazanmai

PLATE 1

Boxes

SCENE 1

YASAKA KAZUKI had three habits that he refused to budge on. Everyone had habits like that, however big or small: things like eating taiyaki from the tail first, washing your arms first in the bath, or starting a mystery novel by reading the ending first. It didn't matter if anyone else understood them; they were absolute and binding.

Kazuki was currently holding a cardboard box in his arms, one that featured the logo of a major international distribution company. Dressed in his breezy school uniform with blue stripes around the sleeves, cradling that ordinary box in his hands as if it were something precious, he began to cross the great bridge that stretched out over the Sumida River.

If someone visiting Asakusa for the first time stood on the red Azuma Bridge and took in the surrounding area, they would be greeted by a strange, mismatched landscape. The Sumida was sandwiched between two wards. On one side was Taito Ward, with its Kaminarimon, or Thunder Gate, numerous historical buildings, and traditional industries. On the other side, where Skytree was located, was Sumida Ward, populated with eccentric, futuristic buildings. The odd sight of the past and future mashed together was normal to Kazuki, who lived in Asakusa for fourteen years now.

Really, there were only three things that were important to Kazuki.

"Good morning! ☆ Every day is happy! And with your lucky selfie, you'll have even more happiness on your plate! It's me, Azuma Sara, dish! ☆"

The Matsuya department store came into view just as he finished crossing the bridge. It featured a large screen, from which drifted the sleepy voice of a girl.

"Here we go! What will be the item for today's lucky selfie?"

The girl on the monitor began to dance to a mysterious tune. She wore a headdress that looked like a plate decorated with a ribbon, and a boldly arranged kimono with a tulle skirt that swayed as she moved. Azuma Sara was a local idol, and this program was named after her—Asakusa Sara TV.

Kazuki froze, eyes intense with emotion as he gazed at the girl on the screen. It was a quiet, special moment, removed from the morning's hustle and bustle.

"Duh-dun! It's a box, dish! ☆ The more boxes you have, the happier you'll be! ☆" A roulette wheel spun, finally landing on a tile with the word "box" written on it. The girl danced around a CG background, surrounded by paper decorations and a cartoon mascot made in her likeness.

The light turned green, and Kazuki continued walking, pushed along by the wave of people.

"...A box, huh?" He glanced at the box in his hands, but just as quickly abandoned the idea. *No, not good enough,* he thought. The more boxes, the better. He couldn't allow himself to compromise his mission.

"You'll have even more happiness on your plate if you send your lucky selfie to someone you care about, dish! ☆ Okay then, have a wonderful day, and may you have lots of luck dished your way!"

"May you have lots of luck dished your way..." he echoed.

Kazuki's wish, unnoticed by anyone else, was meant for only one person.

His three habits were:

1. Walk around holding a box.

2. Check the lucky selfie horoscope.

And finally: 3. Exchange selfies with *that person* every day.

He opened the messaging app on his phone and typed into the conversation box: *It looks like I'll be able to clear today's mission quickly, dish!* ☆ The "dish" and star emoji were tacked on for added charm. He hoped that was forgivable, since there was only one person in the world he'd send such cutesy messages to.

The word "read" appeared beside Kazuki's message, and the child on the other end soon sent him a reply accompanied by a cheerful sticker.

Good morning! ☆ *Let's share happiness with each other today as well!*

That was all the motivation Kazuki needed to do his best today. Honestly, he didn't care if it was sickeningly cutesy; no one else knew about this relationship, and he'd gone into it knowing he could never let anyone find out. But that was fine. It was enough for him to have this connection.

Kuji Toi broke rules, carefully and yet boldly.

The high-rise parking lot, barely spitting distance from Skytree, was largely deserted during the day. A faded sign gently admonished readers to *Beware of Car Vandals*, but that was scarcely enough to persuade Toi to abandon today's prey—a Lexus with a polished sheen that looked entirely out of place in the shabby garage.

He lazily folded back the hood of his black sweatshirt, and then smoothly pulled out a gleaming silver ruler from behind his back. Without hesitating, he jammed the object right into the window frame of the immaculate Lexus.

Bang, clack, bang, bang...Pa-chik!

Wait...Pa-chik?

His hand froze at the absurd sound. Slowly, he twisted around to look in the direction of the noise, only to find a girl standing there in a strange pose. No—it wasn't the pose that was strange. The clothes she wore were fantastical, as if she jumped straight out of a television set. She had a headdress that looked like a plate and a kimono boldly altered to include a mini-skirt. While he admittedly had zero interest in trending fashion, he could tell at a glance that this outfit wasn't normal.

What really caught his attention wasn't the clear distress in her large, round eyes, but the cellphone clutched in her hand.

"You...you took a picture of me just now, didn't you?" His voice flooded with anger, forming words that were less a question than an accusation, one that he was already certain was true.

"I didn't take a picture." Her conflicted expression seemed fragile, somehow, as if she might disappear if he touched her.

But that wasn't important right now.

"Don't play games with me. Give me the phone!" Toi demanded.

"I can't!" Her eyes, formerly sweet as candy, became unexpectedly firm as she refused. She had a Sara mascot strap attached to her cellphone, which bounced as she moved. "I have to complete my mission for *them*, dish!"

Dish? Toi's thoughts froze at hearing that strange word thrown in at the end. The girl used that opportunity to turn and take off running.

"The more boxes, the more happiness, dish!"

Her black hair bounced as she ran, her feathery skirt flipping up to reveal supple thighs and, just a little further up—

No, that's not what he was supposed to be focusing on!

"Stop right there!" Now that he'd finally come to his senses, Toi sped after the girl who was quickly putting distance between them.

"Please, allow me to connect with *them* today as well..." Kazuki whispered.

Before him stood a gleaming, golden statue of a kappa. A kappa might seem an odd choice for a statue, but this was Asakusa's Kappabashi Kitchenware Town. Taito Ward's historical buildings and traditional industries had no shortage of kappa objects that had been left behind over the years, to the point where it wouldn't be an exaggeration to call the area a kappa battleground. But the golden majesty of the kappa enshrined in this plaza gave it an impressive presence, superior to the other, lesser kappa that filled the district.

Why was it gold? And who created it in the first place? No one knew, but at least its appearance gave off the sense it was divine. Kazuki occasionally came here to pray in front of Kappa-sama's statue.

"Hey!" An angry cry rang out through the small plaza.

Kazuki glanced back to find a boy standing at the plaza's entrance, anger and rage obviously thrumming through him.

"Hey, did a girl in a weird outfit come by here?" the boy in the hoodie asked, marching closer one step at a time, a long, narrow weapon gripped in his hand. He was kind of terrifying.

"N-nope," Kazuki replied, completely uninterested in getting involved in the mess. Unfortunately, he then made a vital mistake by readjusting his grip on his cellphone. The strap on it slipped out of his fingers, dangling in the other boy's view—the same strap that *they* had, with the Sara mascot on it.

The other boy's sharp eyes took notice, and his expression darkened even more. "That phone... I knew it, you have some connection with that girl!"

"I-I'm serious, I have no idea who you're talking about!" *Please, make him leave me alone!* Kazuki prayed inwardly. *God, Buddha, Kappa-sama!*

"...I'll run you through!" A sharp, gleaming light slid down the metallic stick in his hand. Kazuki's prayer seemed about to go unanswered as the boy leaped forward to attack, brandishing the weapon.

Fwoosh!

Kazuki escaped by a hair—actually, no, he lost a few as he narrowly managed to evade the first swipe, clinging to the feet of Kappa-sama's statue. That was the second mistake he made that day—and the biggest one of his life.

Krak!

The statue was balanced on one leg, and the ankle of that leg just snapped.

"Whoooa?!"

Bwoooosh!

Kazuki and the broken statue fell in a tangled heap. As soon as they hit the ground, a strange smoke billowed out around them. It consumed the boy in the hoodie as well, filling the entire plaza.

When something unforeseen happens to a person, they nearly always react in the most stereotypical of ways. The two boys were no exception, screaming in unison, "What the heck is thiiiis?!"

When he came to, Kazuki found himself at the back of a classroom, sitting at the desk closest to the window. This was his seat, in his classroom, at his school—Asakusa Sara Junior High.

"It was a dream?" His mind, still in a haze, wandered to the box. Panicked, he whipped his head around, only to discover that his precious box was where he always left it, safely tucked under his desk. "What a relief."

As long as the box was safe, he didn't care whether the whole thing had been a dream or not. Kazuki unconsciously classified things into two categories: things that were important to him and things that weren't. Anything that landed in the former category, he clung to, tight enough to crush them. One might generously call him single-minded, but to put it bluntly, he was obstinate.

"Kazukiiii!"

The person that now entered the classroom didn't fit neatly into either of Kazuki's categories.

Jinnai Enta was the kind of kid who tried to uphold the rules. The entire world seemed to run on rules, and there were consequences for breaking them. In soccer, for instance, which he completely devoted himself to, you could be kicked off the field for violating the rules.

But, right after they finished their early practice this morning, the soccer team's adviser delivered some shocking news.

"What's this about you quitting the team?! You haven't said anything to me about this!" Enta blurted in a rush, still dressed in his practice uniform with a ball in his arms.

"I figured I'd talk to you about it later," said Kazuki.

"What, update me after the fact?! Aren't we supposed to be the Golden Duo? We have been ever since we were kids!"

Kazuki was making that same bitter face he always did when he heard the words "Golden Duo." *Here we go again,* Enta thought.

They'd taken the term from a soccer manga that was popular years ago. Of course, Enta hadn't known about the manga during its publishing run; he spent his childhood overseas due to his parents' jobs. He was pretty sure he only heard about it from his soccer-loving older sister. When he discovered the series, he became enamored with it, and was soon after knee-deep in playing the sport itself.

"Good morning! Homeroom is about to begin!" The boundlessly cheerful voice of their classroom teacher, Jinnai Otone, preceded her into the classroom. This hot-blooded adviser to the Asakusa Sara soccer club was also Enta's older sister. "Ah, hey, Jinnai! Haven't I told you repeatedly to change into your uniform after morning practice?!"

"Ugh, Sis," Enta grumbled. "Now's not the time for that, okay?!"

"That's Ms. Jinnai to you, so long as we're at school!"

"Okay, okay, I'm sorry!" he said, defeated.

"One 'okay' is more than enough, thank you!"

His usual banter with his sister cut off his previous conversation, so Enta reluctantly slunk over and took his seat in front of Kazuki. "I won't accept this, just so you know," he told him, his tone confident and proud, befitting Kazuki's childhood friend.

The truth was, Enta knew deep down that it was unlikely he would be able to change Kazuki's mind. Maybe what he really needed to do was be a more assertive presence in Kazuki's life. But their friendship and his position as Kazuki's childhood friend meant as much to him as soccer; it was a field he didn't want to be kicked off.

"Now, allow me to introduce the new transfer student!" said Otone.

That was odd. Transfer students didn't usually come this late in the year. Enta briefly glanced at the podium but immediately lost interest. A cute girl might have been one thing, but the person standing there was an unsociable-looking boy. He had a black hoodie pulled over his uniform, with a rigid belt and crude lace-up boots. You could tell with one look that he was a delinquent, best to be avoided.

"This is Kuji Toi-kun. Be nice and get along with him, everyone! ♪"

Like that's gonna happen. He's not even interested in greeting us, Enta thought, taking out his irritation from earlier on the transfer student. But then a loud sound rang out behind him.

Ga-thunk!

When he glanced back, he found Kazuki wearing a look of shock as he stared ahead at the podium.

"Kazuki?" Enta said. He had a bad feeling about this. And his bad feelings had a habit of being right.

Both Kazuki and the delinquent uttered the same words, words that were more than enough to plunge Enta further into the pit of foreboding.

"It...wasn't a dream?!"

The boy from Kazuki's dream transferred into the same class as him. If they were a man and woman, this might have set them on the path of a delightfully otherworldly romantic comedy, but the unfortunate reality seemed more like an enemy encounter with a very-much-in-this-world delinquent wielding a ruler. Said delinquent seemed to remember Kazuki's face as well, and the last thing Kazuki wanted was to be blackmailed by him.

Hmm. For some reason his throat felt awfully dry today. During their recess, he purchased a bottle of water from the school canteen, opened the cap, and—

Ching!

A faint, refreshing sound chimed in his ears. *Gluk, gluk, gluk, gluk...*

Kazuki couldn't help the sigh that slipped past his lips after he dumped the cold liquid over the top of his head. "Aahh..."

Beside him, the transfer student from earlier, Toi, was also bathing himself in water at the same time.

"Aaahh..." they both said together.

The otherworldly string of events continued.

Their next period was gym. As Kazuki stood in front of the vaulting box, he heard that sound once again echo in his ear. *Ching!*

In the next moment, both he and Toi stomped hard on the ground, their legs splayed wide apart like sumo wrestlers, chanting, "Dosukoi!"

Enta stared at the two of them as if they were aliens from another planet.

Ching!

The next time Kazuki heard the noise, he was in the school kitchen, chomping on a cucumber. "Otherworldly" no longer did the situation justice; they were entering full sci-fi territory here.

For better or worse, at least he wasn't going through it alone. Toi, the delinquent, had his back pressed against Kazuki's as he munched away on a cucumber, too. The two boys turned at the same time, and their eyes met. In unison, they exclaimed, "Something is calling to us!"

PLATE 1

Boxes

SCENE 2

"TIME FOR THE NEXT news item, dish! ☆ This morning, the kappa statue in the shopping district was found broken. Ka-klink!"

An old woman sat in front of the television—which featured Azuma Sara's offhanded news delivery—with a gaudy bandana wrapped around her head, hands pressed firmly together. The room she occupied was built in the traditional Japanese style: a tatami-floored living space sectioned off by sliding paper doors, leading outside into a vibrant garden. Adorning its interior was a chaotic spread of Asakusa performing arts and soccer memorabilia. The former was her hobby, while the latter reflected the hobbies of her grandchildren—an older girl and a younger boy.

One of those grandchildren was Enta, who was currently mumbling to himself as he gazed down at a box that just arrived. The large exterior box made the tiny one tucked inside seem even smaller. Contained within the latter was a friendship bracelet made of knotted red embroidery floss.

"Ugh. I went to the trouble of buying this, but now what do I do with it? I knew it might take a while, but I really believed he would come back eventually."

When Kazuki first began taking a break from club activities, Enta hadn't pushed him to come back. He tried to be understanding of Kazuki's feelings, but believed that, eventually, time would fix everything.

"Kazuki sure was strange today, though. Was it because of that delinquent transfer student? Actually, it seemed like they knew each other. That jerk, what was he doing going off on his own and getting involved with a creep like that, anyway?"

On the television screen, Sara was getting all pumped up after having shattered a glass bottle. "The Asakusa police don't currently have any leads on the vandals and are still investigating," she said. "Hmph! ☆"

"I bet the culprits will have their shirikodama plucked right out of them by Kappa-sama," the old woman remarked.

Unfamiliar with the term she used, Enta echoed back, "Hm? What's a shirikodama?"

"It's an organ located within a person's anus," his grandmother told him. "Back when I was a little girl, our parents used to warn us that if we were bad, Kappa-sama would come and pluck out our shirikodama."

Enta struggled desperately to imagine his grandmother's "younger years," but his thoughts were interrupted by the sound of Otone throwing open the sliding door.

"Enta! You wasted your money again, didn't you? I see that box. What did you buy this time?!"

"It's not what you think! This is for Kazuki," he explained.

It *would* be his older sister who caught him, of all people. Enta developed a bad habit of spending too much money on online shopping. This was different, though. And now that his sister knew—his nosy, gossip-guzzling, rumor-loving sister—it was only a matter of time before she leaked it to Kazuki. If Enta was going to give him a friendship bracelet, then he wanted to do it on his own terms, when he deemed it appropriate. And that time was *not* right now!

"N-no way..." The menacing look on Otone's face disappeared as her eyes widened in shock, staring at something behind Enta.

He followed her gaze. The box, which had moments ago been sitting atop the tatami, now floated in the air. It whizzed right out of the room and through the garden, disappearing instantly.

"W-wait! That's my box!"

Ching! Ching!

Kazuki and Toi returned to the plaza where they first met that morning. There was no mistake: that strange noise they'd been hearing was definitely coming from here. Yet other passersby seemed entirely deaf to it.

"So no one else can hear it, huh..." Toi mumbled.

"We've been cursed by Kappa-sama," said Kazuki, "for breaking the statue."

"There's no such thing as curses."

The plaza had yellow tape reading "Keep Out" strewn across it, and the area around the broken kappa statue looked like a sectioned-off crime scene.

Ching! Ching!

"If the police catch us, we'll get arrested, won't we?" Kazuki asked.

"The heck am I going to get caught by the cops!"

Kazuki squeezed his box tightly in his arms and shouted back, "I don't want to either! Not if it means I won't be able to connect with *them* anymore!"

Bwoooosh! Suddenly, smoke started spilling from the broken kappa statue's splintered buttocks.

"Something's coming!" Kazuki exclaimed.

"A fart?!"

In the next instant, the statue's beak flapped open, triggering an enormous explosion.

Once again, the two boys screamed in unison, "What the heck is thiiiiis?!"

"Good morning!"

As the smoke gradually cleared away, the haze lifted from their minds.

"We had this same exchange..." Toi began to say.

Kazuki finished, "...this morning."

"I've been waiting for you two, ribbit." Atop the pedestal,

previously occupied by the kappa statue, now stood a new object—a large, white, round piece of mochi. "I am the Kappa Crown Prince, Keppi, ribbit." The strange noise they'd been hearing all day was coming from the mochi, echoing off its head as it struck itself with a cucumber. "I erased your memories of this morning, ribbit."

"You erased our memories?"

"Yes, com-*plate*-ly." The mochi gave a jiggle as it moved, bringing its drowsy eyes and beak into focus.

"Whoa!"

"I can't let you off so easily, not now that you know who I am, ribbit." The words were threatening, but somehow lacked the necessary tension to be effective. The mochi began munching away at the cucumber it was holding.

"Wait, 'ribbit'...?"

"Don't curse us!" screeched Kazuki.

"However...*nomnom*...it must have been fate...*nomnom*...for the two of you to have woken me up...*nomnom*. Thus, I called you...*nomnom*...here again...*gulp*." The mochi extended his legs forward and shockingly prostrated himself before them. "Human children! Please lend me your aid, ribbit! I beg of you, ribbit!"

Kazuki, who was holding his academic good luck charm out as if it were a talisman to ward off evil, paused for a moment. Who would have ever dreamed he'd hear a stock phrase of mecha and magical girl anime thrown at him, here, at Asakusa's Kappabashi?

"Pass," Toi said decisively from beside Kazuki, wielding his silver ruler in hand.

"Huh? Are you sure you want to refuse like that?"

Even though you might be cursed for it? That was the part that worried Kazuki, but Toi was far more pragmatic. He didn't even believe in the existence of kappa.

"See if I care," Toi spat. "Who'd listen to something a frog says anyways?"

"...I'm *not* a frog." The voice crept up in volume from the ground below.

"Huh? A frog?" With those words, Kazuki stepped on a landmine.

"I said that I'm not a damn froooooooog!!" Keppi abandoned his superficial politeness and whizzed up into the air, spinning rapidly as a runaway train on his stubby, plump legs.

"Something crazy's going on!" The two boys turned their backs on Keppi in an attempt to run, finally sensing danger, but before they could flee—

"Desiiiire...Extractioooon!"

—they received a blow to their behinds, the likes of which they'd never felt before. Kazuki's consciousness abruptly cut off.

PLATE 1

ထ

Boxes

SCENE 3

"**H**UH?!"

The next time Kazuki awoke, the sky turned to midnight around him. He heard a pained groaning in the dark, eerie quiet.

"Mmm... Uuungh..." Keppi stood before him, currently in the process of pooping out something roughly the same size as himself. "Mmm... Ahaa..."

Plop...

"Whoaaa! A kappa?!" Kazuki exclaimed. Keppi excreted a kappa wrapped in an amniotic sac. "Kuji became a kappa!"

He could tell that the creature was Toi. How? Well...

"Look who's talking, you're a kappa too!" Just as Toi pointed out, Kazuki became one as well.

"As a prince, it sends me into a rage when people insult me by calling me a frog. So I plucked out your shirikodama, ribbit."

"N-no waaaay!"

Kazuki and Toi both became kappa.

"This is the Desire Field, ribbit. The underside of the human world. Humans can't see kappa or this world, ribbit."

It was as if Kappabashi was submerged under water, for it was cool and dreary, dappled with a scattering of glowing red lights.

"In other words, the two of you are both alive and dead, ribbit."

"Alive...?"

"...and dead?"

The conversation sounded more like fantasy than reality to the two freshly-turned kappa.

"Wait! My box!" A familiar voice called out. Enta was running toward them.

Kappa-Kazuki ran to meet him without thinking. "Enta, it's me!" he cried, but Enta didn't seem to be able to see him at all.

"Leave this to me, ribbit. Here we go... Pfft!" Keppi took out a blowpipe and aimed a shot straight at Enta.

"Gah?!"

The letter "A" appeared on Enta's forehead for a moment before quickly disappearing. Enta blinked for a moment, then gasped. "Wah! It's a huge frog!"

"I'm not a frooooog!" Keppi roared.

"Gyaaaaah!!"

Enta's cry echoed throughout the Desire Field.

In the southern part of Kappabashi Kitchenware Town, two handsome police officers worked in a police box, known only by a handful of people. Despite working in an age of massively popular social networking websites, they remained relatively unexposed to both the goodwill and the contempt of the internet. The Asakusa district was peaceful, and most of their work involved searching for missing pets and handling lost items. Or at least, that was how it appeared.

"Now for our next piece of news, dish! ☆ All across Asakusa, there are reports of a strange phenomenon: boxes flying around under their own power. Bo-box!"

The two officers wore composed expressions on their faces, tuning out the bizarre news program.

When he awoke, Enta, too, had become a kappa. "Huh...?!"

"Tsk, tsk. I've acquired yet another boring shirikodama, ribbit."

Kazuki ignored Kappa-Enta, who still hadn't grasped what was going on, and asked, "What exactly are these 'shirikodama'?"

"It's an organ in a human's body that stores Desire Energy, ribbit."

"Turn us back right now!" Kappa-Toi thundered, unwilling to tolerate this madness any further.

A dark shadow slunk up behind Kazuki and snatched the box out of his hands, then speedily slunk away.

"Ah! That's my box!"

Kazuki looked up to see numerous black, flabby creatures soaring through the air, each with a box in hand. A shining red lamp hung from each creature's head, making the group of them look like a school of deep-sea fish.

"Those are the Kappa Zombies' underlings, ribbit. Humans can't see those either, ribbit."

"My box was flying through the air like that, too!" Kappa-Enta fussed, panicking.

Beside him, Kappa-Toi was secretly losing his composure as well. His precious box was included among those that the underlings—or whatever they were called—were carrying away. "I'll be in big trouble if they open that box..."

"I want to get my box back!" Kazuki exclaimed, unusually emotional.

Keppi said, sounding almost reproachful, "Follow me please, ribbit."

"You three will fight the Kappa Zombies for me, ribbit. They cling to the desires from their previous lives, trying to fulfill them, ribbit."

The red Azuma Bridge, which should have been a familiar sight, had been transformed into a bizarre apparition. Pale, pulsing rings of light surrounded it, and the box-carrying underlings puttered around it. Standing in the middle was a creature, a *thing*, vaguely person-shaped but with an enormous box where its head should have been. The box had both eyes and a mouth, a mouth that chanted the same incoherent phrase over and over again.

"Boxes...boxes...I want boxes..."

If they were to believe Keppi's story, then this "Kappa Zombie" must have possessed a strong attachment to boxes in its previous life. And indeed, the underlings blanketed the bridge in countless boxes. But none of this was relevant to their current predicament; what they really needed to know was how to defeat said monster.

Kappa-Kazuki didn't intend to surrender his box to the creature. Enta and Toi seemed to be of the same mind on that.

"You can destroy a Kappa Zombie by plucking out its shiriko-dama, ribbit. You can extract them as well, now that you've become kappa yourselves, ribbit."

The only route left for the three humans-turned-kappa was to pluck out the Kappa Zombie's shirikodama.

"Now, sing the song!" Keppi commanded.

The moment they heard Keppi's voice, they stopped thinking, and their bodies began to move. Kappa-Kazuki opened his mouth, and a strange song flowed out of him. It was an intense ballad, one he had never heard before, and yet it felt familiar to him, like he'd known it since long ago. Beside him, Kappa-Toi and Kappa-Enta joined their voices to his. As they belted out the lyrics, they felt themselves begin to manifest their full kappa power.

"Kappature it!" As Keppi gave them the signal, the three formed a line with Kappa-Kazuki at the tip, hurtling through the air straight toward the Kappa Zombie's rear.

"Gyaaaaaaah!" The zombie's soul cried out, echoing across the Azuma Bridge.

Kazuki plunged inside the Kappa Zombie's butt. Surrounded by darkness, he squinted his eyes and frantically looked around. It didn't take long before he spotted an orb of pulsating light flying toward him. In case he had any doubts that this was the creature's shirikodama, it had the kanji for 'butt' written across it.

"I've got it!"

With the glowing ball in Kazuki's hands, Toi and Enta, who were holding onto his legs, braced their feet against the edge of the zombie's hole and began to pull.

"Heave!" said Kappa-Toi.

"Damn, he won't budge!" said Kappa-Enta.

The Kappa Zombie frantically clenched his sphincter as tightly as he could to keep them from extracting his shiriko-dama. "Stop it! Don't steal my desire!" If anyone had been watching, they would have witnessed a surreal sight: besides having the lower half of a kappa's body protruding from its butt, the zombie was also leaking a mysterious liquid from the same orifice.

Kazuki refused to give up. "I *have* to pluck out this shiriko-dama! I have to, so I can connect with *them*!"

At the end of their long tug-of-war, the three defeated the creature's sphincter and extracted its shirikodama.

"We kappatured it!" they yelled in unison.

The shirikodama was cool and moist in Kappa-Kazuki's hands. "So this is a shirikodama..."

In a flash, the shirikodama seemed to warp the world around Kazuki. Instead of the Kappa Zombie, an unfamiliar man stood in front of him, one whose face he couldn't quite make out. After a few moments, the man abruptly began to strip. Once the man was completely naked, he took the box that was sitting beside him, one with the logo from that major distribution company on its side. The man turned it over, lifted it up, and gently placed it on his head. The moment he did, Kazuki felt his heart fill with an inexplicable sense of contentment and relief.

Then, just as suddenly, it felt like something inside him was in free-fall, plunging down from his brain to the middle of his chest.

"Now I get it," he said. "You liked getting naked and wearing stolen boxes on your head!"

Goop.

The Kappa Zombie's shirikodama began to melt.

"Ugh?!"

Keppi's resounding voice cut in. "A shirikodama melts when it touches the open air, ribbit! Hurry and transfer it to me, ribbit!"

"T-transfer?! How?!"

As the three panicked, not knowing what to do with the melting shirikodama, Keppi's voice resounded inside their heads again, "*Sarazanmai*, ribbit."

Instinctively, all three shouted loudly.

"Saraaa!"

"Saraaa!"

"Saraaa!"

And then all together, "Sarazanmai!"

As Kappa-Kazuki swallowed the shirikodama, a blinding light radiated out of his body. In the next moment, their consciousnesses seemed to melt like chocolate.

Who could say if it was real or a dream? It was a strange feeling—like becoming one with the universe, as if his body wasn't his own. He wasn't sure if he was Yasaka Kazuki, Kuji Toi, or Jinnai Enta. All three of their consciousnesses were harmonizing in perfect synchronicity. It was as if they were molecules drifting in a hot, primordial ocean, smacking against the thin membranes separating them, and combining into one.

The heat was enough to make him want to scream. The energy was like nothing he'd ever felt before, and the pleasure felt like purifying water welling up beneath his skin. It was like waking up in the morning and being liberated from the pent-up desire that kept you up all night. It was the same sense of ecstasy mixed with shame you got from touching yourself for the first time. It just felt *good*, pleasure so intense that even though you felt unspeakable guilt for experiencing it, was too amazing to quit. Once you knew a world of pleasure like that existed, there was no going back.

The magnetic pull of the Kappa Zombie's shirikodama was so strong that it had no trouble at all dragging out the desire lurking deep within Kazuki's own heart.

"Leaking," they heard Keppi's voice echo.

His consciousness jumped, rewinding back to that morning's events as he had experienced them. It felt like seeing the past recaptured on screen. But there was something none of them understood at the time. Beneath the surface of every event— no, beneath the surface of the whole world—existed a whole other story.

The morning's events, as Kazuki experienced them, began when he was heading to school. After checking Azuma Sara's lucky selfie horoscope, he headed to a children's park with his box in tow. His objective was what stood in the center of the lot—a multipurpose toilet. He entered the handicapped stall and, without missing a beat, began his usual daily routine.

"This is me from this morning?" Kazuki suddenly realized, awakening from his daze. The borders of his body were still fuzzy, and yet he could feel cold sweat pouring from his skin like a waterfall. "Stop it, don't loooook!!"

Unfortunately, without a mouth to speak, Kazuki's cries of protest went unheard, and the reel rolled mercilessly forward.

In the private space of that bathroom, Kazuki abruptly began stripping off his uniform. Then he began to dress himself in an outfit he unpacked from his box. Once the clothes were done, he donned a distinctive pair of red shoes. After that, he pulled on a wig of lustrous, long black hair. Once he smoothed it out with a brush, he puckered his lips and began to apply a thin coat of pink lip balm. His reflection in the mirror looked exactly like Azuma Sara, the idol.

The shirikodama, wrapped up in Kazuki's desire, bled into Toi's consciousness. Sara-Kazuki, on the prowl for that day's lucky selfie item (boxes), wandered inside the garage just in time to witness Toi's vandalism. What followed was exactly the same as Toi remembered from that morning, with one new piece of information: Sara-Kazuki's objective had been the stacks of boxes in the parking lot, not Toi or the crime he'd been committing.

"So *you* were that girl from the garage!" Toi shouted, although his exclamation also produced no sound.

The scene changed once again, the truth about what happened surging through Enta's consciousness like a wave.

Sara-Kazuki managed to lose Toi. He quickly slipped out of his costume and back into his school uniform. He kept an innocent look on his face, box in hand, as he left the multipurpose toilet behind. When he stopped by the Kappa Plaza, he immediately uploaded the selfie he'd taken with his box to the chat window in his phone app, along with a message to *that* person: "Today's lucky selfie mission is complete, dish! ☆"

They responded moments later. "Thanks! I'm so happy every day, thanks to you, Sara-chan, dish! ☆"

"I can't believe it! So Kazuki has been dressing up as Azuma Sara and pretending to be her on a social networking app...?" Enta was similarly unable to give voice to his astonishment, but with their minds merged together, the other two could feel his shock loud and clear.

Equally loud was Kazuki's cry from the heart. "The secret that I couldn't share with anyone... Now everyone knoooooows!!"

The Kappa Zombie's shirikodama now safely transferred. Keppi gulped it down. "Desire consumed."

PLATE 1

Boxes

SCENE 4

"**W**E'RE BACK in our original forms, back to being human! And my box is back too!" Enta's joyful cheer echoed through the Kappa Plaza.

Toi stood there with a disturbed look on his face. His precious box had been returned, now snug in his arms, and the matter was settled. But it was difficult to pass off that profoundly strange experience as nothing more than a dream. The sensations felt all too real. "What was that thing we saw when we were transmitting the shirikodama?"

Keppi sat upon his pedestal, looking sated and satisfied as he answered. "*Buuurp... Sarazanmai* connects your bodies and minds, ribbit. It also means that you share all the secrets you don't want anyone to find out, ribbit."

"So *that* was Kazuki's secret?" Enta asked, his gaze aimed at the entrance of the plaza, where Kazuki sat huddled with his arms wrapped around his legs. His box toppled over beside him, the feminine costume inside it now spilling out onto the ground.

"...That's right," said Kazuki. "I'm a freak that dresses up as Azuma Sara and takes selfies of myself!"

Enta couldn't keep quiet when he heard such shame in Kazuki's tone. "Don't worry about it. I mean, sure, I was surprised, but that's not going to change our relationship at all."

Toi, in contrast, huffed as if he were exasperated. "Are you serious right now? That dude was wearing girls' clothing and posing as an idol!"

"The two of us have a bond that can't be broken so easily!" Enta retorted. "Besides, *Kuji*, breaking into people's cars is a crime!"

"I don't need to be lectured by you."

"What did you say?!" Enta, always hot-tempered, grabbed Toi by his collar.

"Enough, enough, enough!" Kazuki's loud voice stopped them both in their tracks. He started snatching up the pieces of his costume that littered the ground, chucking them back into his box. "I don't need your opinions! I'm not even remotely interested in having you try to understand! This connection is mine alone, *my* connection with *them*! I'll tell as many lies as I need to keep it that way!"

Silence fell in the plaza, one that was interrupted moments later by Keppi. "Now, now, let's all take some time to cool down, ribbit. As thanks for your help today, I'll give you a gift, ribbit." Divine light began to spill from the shell on his back, until the entire plaza was bathed in blinding rays. The shell popped open in a dramatic billow of smoke, revealing a golden plate. "This is a Wishing Plate, capable of granting anything you desire, ribbit. Now listen closely, because what I'm about to say is important, ribbit. This is an incredibly valuable plate that can only be produced by me, the crown prince of the Kappa Kingdom."

"Seriously?!" Enta swiped the plate from him. "Can you get a year's worth of kappamaki with this plate then? Kazuki loves those cucumber sushi rolls!"

The plate, which Enta was brusquely turning over in his hands, flashed with light and the words "A Year's Worth of Kappamaki" appeared on its surface. In the next instant, an enormous cucumber roll came smashing down to the ground.

"Gwah?!"

Keppi hopped up onto the enormous kappamaki and declared, "Your wish has been granted, ribbit."

Ka-klink!

The golden plate cracked and splintered, disappearing without a trace.

"Wait, hold on a second! That didn't count!" Enta hung his head as he tried desperately to gather the fragments in his hands, but it was already too late.

Toi stared, gobsmacked, at the unbelievable scene that unfolded before him. "So what he said was actually true?"

"I would like you all to continue transforming into kappa to pluck out the Kappa Zombies' shirikodama, ribbit. And if you have a wish you would like to have granted, then..."

Kazuki, who watched in silence, only reacted after hearing that last bit.

The world overflows with connections. Blood connections, geographical connections, emotional connections. Everyone is connected in this world.

But those connections disappear easily. I know that better than anyone else.

This time for sure, I have to protect our connection. No matter what it takes.

The Azuma Bridge was so quiet at night. It was hard to believe that until moments ago, it had been crowded with zombies. The light from the bridge's pillars rippled beautifully on the surface of the river below.

Kazuki stood at the river's edge with his box at his feet, the contents of it no longer a secret known only to him. Cradled snugly in his hand was a phone with a Sara mascot keychain attached.

The message on his screen read "Goodnight, Sara-chan."

All he wanted to do was reply with a simple goodnight in return, but his fingers felt impossibly heavy as they tapped across the keyboard. After much struggle, Kazuki finally sent off a short "Goodnight, dish! ☆"

Then he lifted his box and started toward home.

PLATE 1

Boxes

SCENE 5

WHILE KAZUKI AND THE OTHERS slept off their exhausting day, a man pled his innocence to two police officers at the Asakusa Otter police box in the southern part of Kappabashi Kitchenware Town.

"It wasn't me-ow that did it! You've got the wrong purr-son!" He sat at a work desk, facing a number of sorrowful-looking stray cats. A phone, presumably his, lay screen-up on the desk.

One of the police officers, a pale individual with glasses, fixed the man with a sharp glare. The door to the police box snapped shut on its own. The ground below the suspect shifted to show the glowing image of a bright red heart.

"For those souls without beginnings or ends, those unable to connect..." the man with glasses said in a low voice, giving the signal.

"Now, let us open a door..." The other officer, a flamboyant man with blond hair and brown skin, abruptly pointed the barrel of his gun at the suspect.

"Eek?!"

"Is it desire?"

"Or love?"

A mechanical humming came drifting in from somewhere, followed by the beat of a taiko drum that gradually grew louder. It was clear that something terrible was about to happen, yet the man couldn't move.

Without a moment of hesitation, the blond officer pulled the trigger.

"Desire Extraction!"

In the moment after the two policemen exclaimed that phrase, the man's body was nowhere to be found. All that remained was the cellphone on the table. Its pitch-black screen now showed a single, bright red symbol of a heart, with static running across it.

PLATE 2

Cats

SCENE 1

"**I** WOULD LIKE YOU ALL to continue transforming into kappa to pluck out the Kappa Zombies' shirikodama, ribbit. And if you have a wish you would like to have granted, then…"

A voice seemed to echo in Kazuki's ear just before he woke up.

He opened his eyes to a familiar ceiling. He slept on the top bunk of the bed, close enough to the ceiling that he would bonk his head if he tried to sit up. Curtains bordered with red and white hung over the large window beside the bed, but enough light slipped through the cracks to inform him that it would be sunny today.

"A plate that can grant wishes…" He absentmindedly recalled the events of the previous night. Had it all just been a bad dream?

"Kazu-chan!" A cheerful voice called up from below him.

Kazuki slowly lifted himself up. The voice belonged to a little boy who was perched on the bed below, looking up at him. He was Kazuki's younger brother, Haruka. "Hey, for Nyantaro's meal today, do you think we should do Fishtopia? Yesterday was Beeftopia, right?"

Kazuki didn't answer, but just climbed down the ladder and moved to the sliding door. Haruka didn't seem particularly fazed by his lack of response. Instead, he began typing a message into his cellphone.

"Um, let's see... Sara-chan, good morning! Do you like cats? And...send!"

Your average Japanese house had a limited number of places where you could escape from everyone else. Kazuki seated himself firmly on the toilet with his smartphone in hand. The newest message displayed at the top of the chat screen read, *Sara-chan, good morning! ☆ Do you like cats?*

Kazuki immediately set about typing his response. *Good morning! ☆ I love cats, dish! ☆* He hit 'send' and then breathed a sigh.

The header of the chat box read *Harukappa*––Haruka's account name.

Kazuki's life revolved around the daily routine of masquerading as Azuma Sara so he could connect with one particular person. That person was his little brother, Haruka. And it was for Haruka's sake that Kazuki now wanted to obtain the Wishing Plate.

"Good morning! ☆ Every day is happy! And with your lucky selfie, you'll have even more happiness on your plate! It's me, Azuma Sara, dish! ☆" The serene sound of Sara's voice slipped in from the living room television.

"Good morning! ☆ It's me, Harukappa, dish! ☆" Haruka waved his hand at the screen.

"Haruka, stop looking at Sara-chan and eat your food," his mother chided.

"Yes, ma'am!"

"Do they call you 'Harukappa' at school?" his father asked doubtfully.

"Ehehe! That's a secret!"

It was a normal, everyday exchange between family members, one Kazuki eavesdropped on from the other side of the door. He hauled his box out of the room, already dressed in his school uniform. He had to pass by the living room in order to get to the front door. His heart felt heavy just thinking about it.

Despite his efforts to silently sneak past without being noticed, Haruka spotted him anyways. "Oh, Kazu-chan!"

"Morning, Kazu-kun," his mother called. "Breakfast is ready."

It was the same every morning, repeated ad nauseam. There was enough breakfast for four, but Kazuki's answer never changed. "Sorry, I've got to get going."

"All right... Well, take care," she said.

"Wait, hold on! I'm going too!" Haruka hurriedly gulped down his food while Kazuki waited at the entrance for him. This, too, was part of their daily routine.

Their apartment building overlooked the Sumida River. Sumida Park ran along the river's bank, bustling with sightseers, dog walkers, and joggers in the morning. Haruka sat atop the embankment wall of the promenade, feeding Fishtopia to a chubby orange tabby.

"Hey, do you think Nyantaro has put on a bit of weight? She was much slimmer when we first met her, right?"

Kazuki, who was busy checking the lucky selfie horoscope on his phone, replied distractedly, "I doubt she's changed at all."

Haruka laughed, as if recalling their first encounter with the feline. "It made me so happy when you introduced me to Nyantaro. I always wanted a cat, and you were the one who granted my wish!"

"Now then, what will today's lucky selfie item be?" On the screen of Kazuki's phone, Sara watched the spinning roulette wheel until it stopped. "Meeoow! It's a cat, dish! ☆ I love cats, dish! ☆"

As he watched her spin around, holding the plate with the word "cat" written on it, Kazuki felt a wave of relief hit him. "Thank goodness, she really does like—"

"Oh, you're watching Sara-chan! So, you like her too?" Haruka asked.

"Nah, not at all." Those words didn't carry much weight, considering both his phone case and the strap attached to it were Asakusa Sara merch, but he couldn't risk outing himself.

"I love Sara-chan!" said Haruka. "You know, I actually have this really incredible secret, and I'm going to share it with you and only you!"

"Huh? I don't need to hear it."

Kazuki had a bad feeling, so he tried to brush off his little brother's words. Haruka ignored him and continued, "I'm actually friends with Sara-chan. We exchange messages every single day. See?" He beamed as he held up his phone with the chat window open.

Kazuki struggled to sound calm as he asked, "Are you sure you're not just being tricked?"

Haruka was already a fourth year in grade school. It was difficult to believe that he'd been entirely fooled by Kazuki's sloppy cross-dressing. Kazuki was testing him, daring to hint that it was a fake to see how he'd respond.

"I'm not, it's the *real* Sara-chan! Look! See all of these pictures?!" The boy puffed up his cheeks and swiped through the images on his phone. Among the gallery of selfies was Sara with a squid, Sara with a pot, and Sara with some rice.

That's me, and that's me too—they're all me! thought Kazuki. *They're all selfies of me cross-dressing!*

"Ehehe, you're speechless, huh?"

Having confirmed that his younger sibling didn't hold a sliver of doubt about his (or rather, Sara's) identity, Kazuki struck a small victory pose.

In a condo in another part of the city, the constant, rhythmic noise of a running shower acted as a backdrop to the sporadic sounds of a struggle, punctuated by splashes and a hushed groaning. Three men stood in the dimly lit unit bathroom, surrounding a fourth. That man's face was covered by a piece of fabric as he was forcefully shoved down into the filled tub.

One of the men, propped against the wall and wearing a gray suit, asked, "How'd you sniff out this route?" His voice almost sounded bored, disinterested.

"I don't know! I don't know any—bwah!"

The man in the tub wasted his opportunity to speak, so back he went into the water. The person holding him under was a boy in a black hoodie—Toi.

"Tch…" Toi clicked his tongue. The man's legs and arms were bound, but he was a full grown, muscular adult, difficult to restrain. Still, Toi showed the man no mercy. Even when the man was completely submerged and ceased struggling, he didn't let up.

"We don't wanna have to do this to you either, ya know? But if you refuse to talk to us, we got no choice…"

"Bwah!"

Toi loosened his grip and let the man burst back into the air. The drenched captive gasped for air, but then froze as the man in the suit whipped out a glimmering silver object.

"…but to run you through!"

The cold taste of steel shivered on his tongue as the ruler was jammed inside his mouth.

Two black shadows lined up at a water bus stop near the edge of the Sumida River early that morning. One of them was Toi, and the other was the main in the suit. A lollipop protruded from between his lips, at odds with the rest of his attire.

"I swear, you better be careful, you hear? Not like I can come save you all the time."

Toi's slip-up had invited trouble. The morning's events had been an effort to clean it up.

"I'm not going to do something stupid like that again. So take me with you." Toi peered up entreatingly at the man.

The suited man responded only with a look of annoyed exasperation. "We've already talked about this. You'll just get in the way."

Toi expected that answer, but it gutted him more than he anticipated to hear it put so bluntly.

"You understand, right?" said the man. "If this next one goes well, we'll be rolling in money. But if they catch us, it's over."

"If it's money you're after, I can get it!"

For a moment, the man stared back in disbelief. "Hah, you got some guts. If I screw things up, I'll hold you to that, 'kay?"

He wasn't taking Toi seriously at all. It was always like this—he always treated Toi like a child. And now, once again, he was leaving him behind.

The water bus glided up in front of the two.

"Welp, time to fly. Don't do anything stupid, you get me?" The suit-clad man tousled Toi's hair.

He should've batted the man's hand away and told him, "I'm not a kid anymore!" But Toi never could bring himself to do that.

"You too, bro," Toi called after him.

Chikai, his older brother, disappeared onto the boat. They wouldn't see each other again until his brother successfully finished his next task. They shared a promise for the distant future, but there were no guarantees in the present.

Toi had no intention of sitting around in the interim. He intended to get his hands on a Wishing Plate—for his brother's sake.

"Time for our next piece of news, dish! ☆ This morning a man's remains were discovered by the Sumida River. Riveer~! ☆"

An elderly woman sat in front of a television set, a colorful bandana wrapped around her head, watching as Azuma Sara gave a carefree delivery of some grave news.

Her grandson, Enta, was nearby, opening the box he worked so hard to retrieve the night before—the one that had Kazuki's present nestled inside of it. At least that's what was supposed to be inside of it.

"What the heck is thiiiiiis?!" he instinctively howled, backing away. "This isn't my box... Wait, does that mean this is Kuji's...?"

"Enta!"

"Eek! Sis, don't scare me like that!" He hid the package behind his back as Otone eyed him suspiciously.

"What are you yelling about? And have you been ordering stuff online again?!"

"No! This is Kuji's, I accidentally grabbed it," Enta explained.

"Oh, wow. You two are getting along that well, huh?"

"The heck we are! That bas...I mean, Kuji's a dangerous guy!" *I can't let that punk get any closer to Kazuki,* Enta thought.

Inside the box behind him was a gleaming, silver handgun.

PLATE 2

Cats

SCENE 2

ENTA COULD BARELY FOCUS during the school day, and when it was over, he used the excuse of a stomach ache to skip out on club activities. Now, he was standing at the front gate. Frankly, he wanted to consult Kazuki about the gun situation sooner, but since Toi was seated directly beside Kazuki, Enta had lost his nerve every time he looked back to try. His only option now was to catch Kazuki on his way home.

"It's not like I'm scared of Kuji or anything. It's just awkward and inconvenient to have him sitting close by when I'm trying to talk. Last night I just went with the flow, but I never liked him in the first place. I need to make sure that Kazuki never hangs around him again."

As Enta mumbled to himself in anguish, Kazuki passed right in front of him with a box cradled in his arms.

"Wait, Kazuki!" Flustered, Enta chased after the other boy, swerving around him so he was facing Kazuki.

"Enta?"

"Uh, hey, there's something I want to talk to you about."

"Sorry, I'm in a hurry right now. Let's talk tomorrow."

"Huh? Hey, w-wait!"

Kazuki began walking off, leaving a dumbfounded Enta behind.

"What the heck?! I thought we were supposed to be the Golden Duo?!"

Behind the wailing Enta, Toi exited the school gate and started walking in the opposite direction. Without, of course, sparing a glance Enta's way.

One of Asakusa's most famous tourist spots was Japan's oldest amusement park, Hanayashiki. It was crammed onto a tiny strip of land and jam-packed with a whole array of attractions. Its main attraction was a roller coaster, the oldest in Japan. Although there were other roller coasters touted as "the fastest," "the tallest," and "the most fear-inducing," this one was a contender for the most thrilling. Just stopping and thinking about how old it really was could induce an adrenaline high. But there was also one curve where the track pressed terrifyingly close to a wall lining the boundary of the park. It felt like one wrong move would send you crashing right into it.

This was the wall that Toi was walking along now.

The interior of the park, with its echoes of cheerful laughter, stood in stark contrast to the exterior, with its distinct, foreboding aura. Toi had his black hood pulled up over his head and his jacket zipped all the way shut as he navigated the maze of residential complexes to a certain building. Inside, he strolled up to the elevator entrance, bumping the button with the middle knuckle of his index finger. After the doors eventually slid open, he stepped in and immediately pressed the "close doors" button with the same knuckle. Then he pressed several of the numbers on the pad.

He'd seen his brother do the same long ago and asked the purpose of it. His brother responded, "This way, they won't be able to follow you." Now, he didn't even have to think about it. His body just moved automatically. It was little habits like this that made Toi feel connected to his brother.

He disembarked from the elevator and walked soundlessly to a room at the end of the hallway. When he quietly tried the door, it swung open to reveal a room lit with bright, purple growing lights. Tall plants with broad, five-fingered leaves lined the floor. Others hung upside down along the wall, drying in front of the ventilator. A desk was squeezed into the space, atop which sat some powder, ground down from the plants' buds.

Toi slipped on his usual mask and thin plastic gloves, now firmly in work mode. In this secret room, he began dividing the dried marijuana and stuffing it into bags. To further camouflage them, he then tucked several of the tiny packets into a bag with cat food packaging on it.

This was the biggest source of Toi's income. His clients were all regulars he inherited from his brother. He never sold to the same person twice in one month. He never met them directly. Toi was careful not to rouse suspicion, and had taken several other meticulous measures to avoid notice as well.

And yet someone sniffed out his route, and he'd inconvenienced his brother as a consequence. Now he was desperate to try to recover from his failure.

The flip phone he used for business began to vibrate—an order from one of his customers.

"Yeah, no problem. I got some exceptionally high-quality stuff right now. The pickup will be at..."

If he made this work, he would be one step closer to living with his brother. No sooner had he thought that than—

Thunk!

—something heavy slammed against the top of his desk.

"Huh?"

"Mreeow?"

When he ended the call and looked back, Toi found a chubby orange tabby with one of the packages he'd just finished sealing—the word *Fishtopia* stamped across the front—clamped inside its mouth.

A cat?

The two stared each other down, but it was the cat who moved first.

"Mreow!"

Despite its chubby physique, the cat was unbelievably agile as it slipped past the plastic sheet hanging around the perimeter of the room, and then leaped out the small crack in the open window. And, of course, it took the cat food bag with the freshly packed weed still inside it.

"Dammit! Wait right there, you stupid cat!" Toi yelled loudly after it, scrambling noisily as he jetted out of the room.

"Strange, I don't see a single cat around here."

As was his daily routine, Kazuki was dressed as Azuma Sara and searching for the lucky selfie item of the day. He could usually complete a mission this simple immediately after school let out, but this one was proving to be harder than expected.

"I figured a cat would be a piece of cake to find—whoa!" Something slammed into his back, pitching him forward. "That hurt..."

"Mreow!" The culprit was an orange tabby.

"Nyantaro?! Don't surprise me like that. Although...maybe the two of us can come to an agreement here." As Sara-Kazuki approached, ready to snap a selfie, the cat began desperately screeching at him.

"Mreow! Mreeeow!"

"Huh? Where'd you get that Fishtopia bag from?" Kazuki wondered.

"I found you, you fat-ass cat!"

"Kuji?" Kazuki glanced back to find a ruler-wielding Toi standing there, looking absolutely furious. It felt like déjà vu.

Toi completely ignored Kazuki and his Sara cosplay, and swiped his weapon at the animal, ripping through the bag it was carrying. "Give it back! Or I'll run you through!"

Panicked, Kazuki inserted himself between the two. "Knock it off! This cat is really important to Haruka and me!"

While the two yelled at each other, the cat in question began to sniff at the small packets that tumbled onto the ground.

"Just shut up and move it!" Toi shouted. "Huh?"

"Mreeeoow." With a gulp, the cat swallowed up one of Toi's precious packages of weed.

"You've gotta be kidding me! I'll slice your stomach open!"

Toi began whipping his ruler wildly through the air. Sara-Kazuki struggled desperately to hold him back, yelling to the cat, "Nyantaro, run for it!"

"Mreow!"

"As if I'll let you get away!"

Thus began the Great Asakusa Chase.

"Damn that Kazuki. How does he expect me to handle this all by myself?"

Elsewhere in the city, Enta walked down a street with Toi's box in his hands, still fuming over being turned away by Kazuki earlier.

"Guess I should go to the police. That'd be the normal thing to do in this situation, right?"

Isn't there a police box near the entrance to Kitchenware Town? I guess I'll just go there. Just as he thought that, though, something reached out and snatched him by the ankle.

"Gah!"

Enta was yanked inside the Kappa Plaza, where he discovered Keppi, shriveled and covered in sweat. The deflated mochi was lying on his side on the statue's pedestal, his arm outstretched, clinging to Enta's foot.

"I'm dying of starvation... Save me, ribbit."

"What do you think you're doing, Keppi?! I don't have time for this right now!"

PLATE 2

Cats

SCENE 3

"**M**REEEEOW," said the cat. Behind her, the symbol of Hana-yashiki Park, Bee Tower, jutted up toward the sky.

"Quit running all over the place and get down here!" called Toi, brandishing his ruler at the cat as it stood on a rail up above him.

Sara-Kazuki intervened once he caught up. "Nyantaro, run!"

"You jerk, quit getting in my way!" Toi barked at him.

"I *will* get in your way!"

The cat took the opportunity to make her escape, disappearing over the other side of the railing and into the park. Toi scrambled for the park entrance with Sara-Kazuki hot on his heels. "Don't follow me!" he yelled back at the other boy.

"I *will* follow you!"

The competition was fierce, and yet, both of them froze in their tracks at the entrance. There, they both gazed up silently at the oversized sign hanging over the entrance.

Couples Only Today! ♡ *Hosting a Lovey-Dovey Bee Ninja Festival!*

In smaller text below: *Only Couples Allowed* ♡

55

Apparently, the park was trying to increase its weekday visitors by holding unique events like this.

"...Let's do this tomorrow instead," Toi proposed.

"Yeah, good idea," Kazuki agreed.

Just as they turned to leave, a hand reached out and grabbed both of them.

"Nin! Nin!" exclaimed the man locking each of them in place.

"Wha?!" They both gaped in surprise.

"Allow me to escort our next lovey-dovey couple!"

By the time they realized what was happening, it was already too late; an all-too-eager park assistant, decked out in a ninja outfit, was forcibly dragging them inside the park.

"Delicious, ribbit~! ♡ Delicious, ribbit~! ♡" Keppi poured the bottle of cucumber-flavored Shirohasu mineral water—which he forced Enta to purchase and bring to him—over the top of his head. Gradually, he returned to his former, rotund self.

"Yeah, yeah. Glad to be of service, ribbit," Enta muttered. "Jeez. Kazuki's just left me on read, as usual. What should I do?"

"*Buuurp*! Now's not the time to dilly-dally, ribbit. Seeds of evil are taking root in the city right at this very moment, ribbit."

"Hm? 'Seeds of evil'...?"

Beep-beep!

Enta's phone chirped. "Kazuki?! Ugh, it's just my sister..."

It was a selfie of Otone and her boyfriend on a date at Hanayashiki. He had to wonder if it was even professionally appropriate for her to be sending such a picture to one of her students—even if that student was also her little brother. "Some people sure do have it good, out there having fun, oblivious to the suffering of others," Enta sighed.

"You said it, ribbit. Those two have a duty to defeat the Kappa Zombies, but they don't seem to appreciate our impending crisis, ribbit," Keppi commented, peeking at Enta's phone.

"Wait, what two?" Enta narrowed his eyes and searched the photo. There was Otone, beaming like the protagonist of a 90s shoujo manga, with her boyfriend hugging her from behind. In the background, he could see a couple perched on a kids' ride. "Is that...Kuji and Kazuki?!"

Long ago, before Hanayashiki's mascot was Panda Car, it was Bee Boy, originally known as Bee-chan. Few people nowadays remembered the origin of Hanayashiki's symbolic Bee Tower, or the Bee Boy symbol stamped on it.

Kazuki's appearance gathered a fair amount of confused looks as he walked about the park. On top of his Azuma Sara disguise, he wore a bee antenna headband, stylized black ninja garb, bee wings on his back, and a large, striped stinger on his butt.

"Today's lovey-dovey couples will dress up as bee ninjas and must keep their hands interlocked at all times," they were told. It was a bee-ninja couple cosplay event.

Kazuki stared vacantly at Toi's back as the other boy walked ahead of him. The latter entered the park reluctantly in pursuit of the cat, and adamantly refused to participate in dressing up. After a verbal altercation with the park assistant, Toi compromised, wearing the bee part of the costume over his usual black hoodie. The result looked ridiculous, like a gag costume someone might wear after losing a bet. Kazuki found the half-baked disguise utterly embarrassing.

"There he is! That fat cat!" Toi flew after the feline, letting go of Kazuki's hand.

Kazuki snapped back to his senses and charged after the other boy. How many times were they going to do this? Every time Toi let go of his hand, it only resulted in—

"You there, the lovey-dovey couple! Holding hands is proof of your love! You must hold hands at all times!" The ninja-garbed assistant blew his whistle in warning at them.

Kazuki caught up with Toi and yanked his hand, grinning at him. "I'm so sorry I let go of your hand, dish. ☆ My darling. ♡"

"Let go of me!"

"Couples that don't hold each other's hands get forcibly removed from the park!" the park assistant snapped at Toi.

"...Tch."

With that, the (not so) lovey-dovey couple resumed their handholding as they hunted down the elusive cat through the park's attractions. After a substantial amount of time spent searching in vain, they ended up riding the Sky Ship.

"And now our lovey-dovey couples will be guided on a trip through the sky!" the assistant announced airily.

Kazuki and Toi found themselves gliding through the air on a boat decorated with hearts. In front of them, Nyantaro trotted unconcernedly along the upper rail.

"Nyantaro! Hurry, run!" Kazuki called after him.

"Hey, you, enough of that already!"

"That cat helped Haruka and me connect with each other."

"Who the heck is Haruka?" Toi asked. "Your lover?"

"Haruka's my...beloved younger brother." The beloved younger brother that he deceived by pretending to be an idol. As the words left his lips, Kazuki averted his eyes. Despite the rush of guilt that welled up in him, he just really wanted to see Haruka smile. There was no repaying the debt he owed Nyantaro for bringing them closer.

"I can give up on the cat then," Toi mumbled.

"Really?!"

"But in exchange...give me any Wishing Plates we get."

After a brief pause, Kazuki said, "That I can't do!" He couldn't give up on securing a Wishing Plate—not even to guarantee Nyantaro's safety. Those plates were the only way for him to make his long-held desire a reality.

"Quit being so selfish about everything!" Toi snapped at him.

"You're one to talk! What do you have against Nyantaro anyway?!"

As the two quarreled, keeping their hands firmly locked together, the cat in question disappeared.

Sarazanmai

PLATE 2

∞

Cats

SCENE 4

AN IMPOSING HUSH settled over the large conference room at the Asakusa Police Station, where a meeting was presently underway. A sign on the outside of the door read *Asakusa Suspicious Death Investigation HQ.*

The chief's voice echoed inside the dimly lit room. "We have identified the body we found early this morning. Thirty-eight-year-old unemployed Nekoyama Moukichi." The profile revealed that the deceased's name included the kanji for "cat" and "fur." "Six months ago, he was arrested as a suspect in connection with the Asakusa Cat-Skinning Case, where someone captured strays and flayed their bodies. He was released after we failed to bring charges against him. We'll be investigating his death as a homicide."

There was an audible *ka-chik* as the projector flipped to the next image on the slideshow. One was an image of the cats in question, initially gathered as evidence. The scenes depicted were too gruesome for any feline enthusiast to behold. The prevailing mood in the room was clear; it wouldn't be surprising for someone to hold a grudge against the perpetrator of such a brutal crime.

In the midst of all of this, two people abruptly stood up. It was the two police officers from before.

"We're the ones who took care of him!" said the blond one.

"It was just yesterday!" said the one with glasses.

Yesterday evening, to be precise. The incident took place at the police box where the two worked.

"It wasn't me-ow that did it! You've got the wrong purr-son!"

"For those souls without beginnings or ends, those unable to connect..." The man in the glasses, Akutsu Mabu, held up a photo that showed Nekoyama at the scene of the crime, hauling a cloth bag stuffed full of cats he kidnapped.

"Now, let us open a door..." The blond officer, Niiboshi Reo, suddenly aimed the barrel of his gun at the man. "Is it desire?"

"Or love?"

A large taiko drum appeared above Nekoyama's head.

"Desire Extraction!"

Nekoyama was instantly absorbed into the drum and disappeared completely.

Bam!

Accompanied by the thundering of the drum, the floor of the police box began to descend downward. The captured man was stuffed inside a box, and then sent along a conveyor belt along with numerous other boxes, carried into the depths of an enormous underground structure. Each box was sealed along the way with the stamp of a red heart. As the boxes began to pile up in the hundreds, a red crane suddenly descended out of nowhere, seizing the towering pile and carrying them off.

"Don't let go of your desires!"

"Wring out desire!"

Reo and Mabu danced together down to the innermost depths of the building. In a dimly lit room, a taiko drum hovered in the air, wrapped in rings reminiscent of the planet Saturn's. Nekoyama Moukichi's captured body began to transform as the rings pulsed with light.

Reo ripped Mabu's shirt open across his chest. Deep beneath Mabu's pale skin, a gray, glowing heart trembled violently in response. Reo didn't hesitate; he sank his fingers into the other man's pale chest. It spasmed, as it always did. Not a single drop of blood spilled as Reo wrapped his hand around Mabu's heart. Mabu's mechanical heart flashed with blinding light: a sign that the two of them were connected.

Reo was unmoved by Mabu's ecstasy as he vigorously yanked the organ out of the other man's chest. The room's darkness filled with a vibrant red, like the crimson petals of a flower only the two of them could bring to blossom.

Sarazanmai

PLATE 2

∞

Cats

SCENE 5

NYANTARO LAY ACROSS THE ROOF of one of the candy houses dangling from Bee Tower, fast asleep, a bubble of snot protruding from her nose.

"What the heck are you doing there?!" Toi, who kept his fingers threaded with Sara-Kazuki's this whole time as the latter fussed over the feline's well-being, was becoming increasingly fed up. "Hey, fat cat! You wait right there, I'm going to go over there and snatch you up!"

The cat jumped up, as if sensing Toi's hostility, the snot bubble giving an audible pop as it burst. "M-mreow?!" Seeming to forget just how high up she was, she leaped off the edge of the roof—and began to plummet tens of meters to the ground below.

"Nyantaro!" cried Kazuki.

The inevitable tragedy flashed through both boys' minds. But, mere inches from the ground, Nyantaro's body suddenly froze. The next moment, she began rotating in circles as she levitated off toward the Azuma Bridge. It was just like what happened with the boxes the previous night.

"Could this be...?" began Toi.

"No way..." added Kazuki.

Suddenly they heard Keppi's voice behind them. "This is the work of those Kappa Zombies, ribbit!"

"Kazuki! Are you all right?!" Enta blurted.

The other boy was dressed in a ninja bee outfit as well, holding hands with Keppi, who was dressed as a Japanese courtesan.

Fwooosh...

A sudden gust of wind carried off Keppi's kimono singlet. The Kappa Crown Prince was left balancing on a couple of bamboo stilts with only his gaudy make-up still intact, his chest puffed out to resemble a woman's.

Sara-Kazuki was shocked into speechlessness until the sound of an incoming message brought him back to his senses. It was an SOS from Haruka.

Harukappa: Sara-chan, big trouble! Nyantaro has gone missing!

"Haruka's asking for help!" he said.

Toi stared in the direction they'd last seen the tubby feline flying, and venomously spat, "I need that weed so I can make money!"

"You can fix everything by becoming kappa and extracting the Kappa Zombie's shirikodama, ribbit."

"No, we can't!" said Enta. "Kuji! Don't get any closer to Kazuki!"

"Enta...?"

Enta turned to his confused friend and explained, "Listen to me, Kazuki, that punk was carrying this kind of dangerous weapon around!" He held out a worn Tokarev TT-33. It was unmistakably Toi's gun.

"Bastard, where the heck did you... Just give it back!"

"No way!" Enta snapped back.

"That's not something you should be carrying," Toi warned.

"Like I care! Anyway, get away from Kazuki!"

"Everyone..." Kazuki began, breaking the silence he maintained while the others argued. "We all have things we can't talk about. I want to save Nyantaro, for Haruka's sake. And I need Kuji to be able to do that!" He looked Enta straight in the eye, giving the latter no choice but to bite his tongue.

Kazuki willingly bent his butt toward Keppi and braced himself as the kappa-like creature took the plunge.

"Desiiiiiire...Extraaaaction!"

A rickshaw went flying down a street, whizzing by shop fronts and a Shinto shrine.

"Let's combine our dishtopian strength and plate this zombie, ribbit!"

"So I guess we're doing the shirikodama relay again," Kappa-Enta mumbled.

Kappa-Toi ignored him in favor of asking, "Are we gonna have our secrets revealed like last time?"

"Battle always entails risks, ribbit."

"No matter what happens, I *will* save Nyantaro!" declared Kappa-Kazuki.

"Kappature it!"

Cats were the object of this zombie's desire. A desire, Kazuki discovered once he extracted the shirikodama, born from rejection when the man's cat-crazy girlfriend became so obsessed with felines that she chose them over him.

I want to be a cat. He could hear the man's inner thoughts. *I'm so jealous. I wish she'd play with me, too...*

Kazuki could feel the man's satisfaction as he fantasized about wearing a suit made of cat fur, sleeping peacefully on his girlfriend's lap, lost in a world of dreams.

"So that's it. You wanted the person you cared about to love you. That's why you collected all of that cat fur, so you could become a cat yourself."

"Oh no, you found me-owt!"

"Saraaa!"

"Saraaa!"

"Saraaa!"

And then all together, "Sarazanmai!"

They were familiar enough with the process on this, their second time, that they spent only a few moments drifting in the waves of pleasure. And almost immediately afterward, Keppi's voice echoed.

"Leaking."

Kazuki had been the one to pluck out the shirikodama, so once again it was his secret being leaked. He had mentally prepared himself for the possibility, which did little to make the situation more palatable.

The three shared the same mental image of the Yasaka house-hold's living room. On the television, a couple of adorable kittens were playing with each other. Haruka watched them eagerly, while Kazuki sat beside the other boy with a look of disinterest on his face.

"Aww, they're so cute...I hope we can have a cat someday."

Pets were prohibited in the condominium where Kazuki and his family lived.

"A cat, hm..." Kazuki eyed his little brother and the television as he concocted a plan in his mind.

The scene changed, revealing a luxurious home with an expansive lawn. Kazuki stood in front of the mansion, his gaze focused on a gaudily dressed Nyantaro.

"Yasaka and that fat cat? What's he doing?" Toi's suspicions were soon answered.

Kazuki approached the terrace where Nyantaro (actually called Elizabeth at the time) was sunbathing. He snatched up the feline, and then ran for his life. A few days later, as Haruka sat at the river's edge, Kazuki approached him with the cat in his arms.

"Look, it's one of the local strays! Her name is Nyantaro."

"Oh wow! So cute!!"

The cat now had a small chunk missing from one of its ears, usually a clear indicator of a stray. The one on Nyantaro, however, was something Kazuki had done himself.

"Kazuki, you stole someone's cat and forced it to become a stray?!" Enta's voice trembled with emotion, shocked by Nyantaro's secret origin.

"That's right," Kazuki admitted. "I did it to make Haruka happy!"

"Desire Extraction!"

As the Desire Field dissipated across town, the two police officers, Reo and Mabu, were riding an elevator deep inside their underground lair.

"It appears we have some meddlers." Mabu held a familiar photograph in his hand—the one with Nekoyama at the scene of the crime. As they watched, the man disappeared from the picture.

Reo quirked a brow and said softly, "Let's hurry. Only those who can connect to their desires have the ability to grasp the future in their hands."

The elevator soared endlessly upward, giving off an eerie hum as it went.

Back at the Kappa Plaza, Nyantaro was safe and sound—perched atop the cement statue stand and straining over her makeshift litter box. Apparently, she hadn't found the opportunity to relieve herself amid the day's adventures. Cats were naturally prone to constipation, especially overweight ones like Nyantaro. In front of the feline, an awkward silence settled between Enta and Kazuki, the latter holding a plate he'd just received from Keppi.

"Um, hey. I get that Haruka is really important to you, but it seems kinda wrong to steal someone's cat. I feel bad for Nyantaro, too, considering you injured her when you—gwah?!" Enta went flailing forward after being kicked from behind. "What the heck?!" He looked up and found himself staring down the barrel of a lead-colored gun.

Toi held the weapon, a plastic bag dangling from his gun hand and a box in the other. "Someone steals from you, you take back what's yours. And I'm taking this bag of weed."

The contents of said bag were likely the cause of Nyantaro's constipation.

Toi threw the box at Enta, who was still frozen from having a gun turned on him.

"Hey, this is mine!" Inside was the friendship bracelet Enta purchased. He mistakenly switched boxes with Toi during all the commotion the night before.

"Just be glad I didn't toss it," Toi huffed. Next, he turned his gun on Kazuki. "Now hand over that plate."

"No!"

Having anticipated that answer, Toi quietly said, "You and I aren't so different. We're the kind of people who'll do anything to get what we want."

The accuracy of that statement struck Kazuki speechless, but Enta cut in to cover for him. "Kazuki wants to use that plate for his little brother! He's not like you!"

"Ah yes, I forgot to mention something, ribbit." Keppi interrupted once again, standing atop his bamboo stilts as he said, "The plate I bestowed upon you this time is a silver Wishing Plate. You'll require five of these in order to have your wish granted, ribbit."

"What the?! You could've told us that sooner!" seethed Enta.

Toi dropped his gun and turned to walk away. "I'll get the next one."

Kazuki had a bitter look on his face as he watched the other boy leave. "Still, for Haruka's sake, I have to…"

Sara-Kazuki and Nyantaro sat together at the edge of the Sumida River. He had the chat window open on his phone, having just sent his selfie with the feline a few moments ago.

"Phew. I managed to finish today's mission."

So much had happened that day. Kazuki was exhausted from all of the running around.

His phone rang with a *bing* as Haruka's reply came in.

Harukappa: Nyantaro! I'm glad she's safe!

Harukappa: I just knew it. Your selfies really do bring good luck!

"I'm so glad it's over." Kazuki sighed with relief, and a strong wave of exhaustion washed over him. Nyantaro was snoozing away next to him, so maybe he could grab a few winks as well. Sara-Kazuki shut his eyes as the gentle trickle of river water lulled him into a deep sleep.

At the water's edge, beneath the glistening night sky, a dark shadow appeared over the sleeping Kazuki. Nyantaro woke, sensing their presence. "Mreow?"

The feline's round cat eyes watched as Enta leaned down to plant a kiss on the unconscious Kazuki.

PLATE 3

Kiss

SCENE 1

I T WAS A BRIGHT Sunday morning. In the Jinnais' living room, Enta's grandmother sipped her tea as she always did. Across from her sat Otone, decked out in fishing gear, polishing her rod as she yelled, "Entaaa! Breakfast!"

The television behind the old woman was tuned to its usual channel, Asakusa Sara TV. It was almost time for the lucky selfie horoscope segment to begin.

"Morning..."

Enta stifled a yawn as he entered the room, still dressed in his summer pajamas. He hadn't slept at all the night before. He plopped himself down at the floor table, only to wrinkle his nose in disgust when he caught sight of breakfast. "Ugh, fish *again*?"

He skillfully snapped up the fish in his chopsticks and dangled it in the air, its body split wide open to reveal the finely cooked meat inside.

Otone said sharply, "Kiss!"

"Kiss?!" he shrieked back, instinctively dropping the fish.

Why—how does she know?!

Otone, having noticed how flustered her brother was, casually added, "Not kiss, I said kisu. You know, the fish? Sillago? We dried it overnight."

"Huh? O-oh, the fish... I panicked for a second there." Enta regained his composure and returned the fish to the plate. "Is this another present from that boyfriend of yours?"

"That's right. My attractive, picture-perfect boyfriend who's a master at preparing fish. I'm off in a few to go on another fishing date with him!" Despite her tomboyish appearance, Otone lived for romance. Romance, she claimed, gave her energy to get through the day. She seemed to glow as she talked about her boyfriend.

Although Enta was used to her gushing, he found it especially annoying this morning. Annoying enough that he was tempted to take a dig at her. "I just wish your boyfriend worked at a butcher's instead of the fish market."

"That's uncalled for! If this were soccer, I'd give you a yellow card!" Otone huffed.

Enta ignored her and lifted his miso soup bowl to his lips. On the television, Sara's lucky selfie roulette wheel came to a stop.

"Smooch, smooch! It's a kiss, dish! ☆"

"Bwah?!" Enta choked, spewing his soup.

"Did you hear that? A kiss! Maybe he'll kiss me today on our date?! Or maybe I should be the one to initiate it? Hee!"

As Otone prattled and Enta coughed, the girl in the television smiled and said, "Okay then, have a wonderful day, and may lots of luck be dished your way! ☆"

While the tunnel beneath the west side of the Azuma Bridge remained unobstructed, the east side tunnel was sealed off completely. This made it an optimal spot for Enta's training; there was barely any foot traffic, and the area was spacious.

His Sunday schedule was practically a fixed routine by now. After eating breakfast, he would come here, clean up any trash he found, and then begin training with the soccer ball he brought with him. He was normally so engrossed in training that he'd lose track of time juggling the ball on his legs. Today, however, he felt too gloomy to concentrate the way he usually did.

He sighed and glanced back at the sealed tunnel. A picture of a soccer goal had been painted onto the stone wall. He approached, ghosting his fingers over the lines. The painting was four years old now, and was beginning to peel and fade.

I love Kazuki, he thought. *I don't remember when it started, but it's like I've carried these feelings with me forever. I refuse to accept that Kazuki's quit soccer.*

At ten years old, Enta stood out in school. He'd spent the better part of his childhood living overseas, thanks to his parents' jobs. His older sister was so charismatic she could make friends anywhere, regardless of language barriers. Enta, on the other hand, was incredibly shy. He constantly cried to his concerned parents that he wanted to go back home to Japan.

He managed to hitch a ride back a few years later with his sister, who said she wanted to get a teaching license, and they moved to Asakusa to live with their grandmother. Instead of a happy homecoming, Enta's classmates were reserved and aloof toward him—a familiar situation to most Japanese children returning from abroad. Perhaps they were merely curious about him and his background, and Enta misinterpreted their intentions. Regardless of whether it was a misunderstanding, it broke the introverted boy's heart.

After school, Enta always sat in a shady spot overlooking the school grounds, where he could read his soccer magazine in peace. The boisterous sounds of his classmates playing soccer carried easily to him. Enta was too shy to approach and ask to play. He was left with no choice but to hug his knees to his chest and watch. He'd always played by himself when he lived abroad, so it wasn't like he knew how to be part of a team anyway.

Kazuki was the one who finally outstretched a hand to him. When he told Kazuki that he loved soccer but was only a beginner, the other boy smiled and responded that he just started playing too.

"I'm sure we can become a golden duo someday, just like the characters from that manga!" Kazuki said. The other boy wore a blue friendship bracelet tied around his right ankle, the same kind worn by Enta's favorite soccer player.

Enta accepted his outstretched hand and from there, they began practicing daily, just the two of them. Soon after, they discovered this empty area near the base of the Azuma Bridge. The two young boys painted a small soccer goal on the stone, and it became their secret practice field.

They were recognized (by both themselves and others) as the "Golden Duo," in part thanks to Otone's influence as she had trained to become a junior high P.E. teacher. They even had a special pose they would both strike during matches after Enta passed the ball and Kazuki scored. It was the pose their favorite soccer player always used. Their motto was, "Dishing it out!"

Several months ago, however, Kazuki decided to leave soccer behind. The blue friendship bracelet on his right ankle disappeared at the same time. Enta, wanting to respect his friend's feelings, watched and said nothing as Kazuki stopped participating in the club. He was sure that Kazuki just needed a break, and would come back to the club eventually.

Kazuki and I have been the Golden Duo ever since we were little, he thought. *I know him better than anyone else. I want to pass to him and watch him score again.*

Enta produced a small box from his pocket. It was a new friendship bracelet he bought for Kazuki. Just when he planned to gift it to his friend, Kazuki submitted his club withdrawal form.

"Once Kazuki fulfills his wish using the Wishing Plates, I can give him this and we can go back to being the Golden Duo again. I don't need anything else but that."

Images from his kiss with Kazuki the night before popped into his mind. Kazuki awoke right after but had no memory of what Enta had done. Enta should've been relieved that he hadn't been caught, but a part of him felt disappointed. That was probably why he'd taken out his frustration on Otone this morning.

Looking at his sister—the way she loved unapologetically and faced everything head on—was like looking straight at the sun. She was too bright. Of course, that often led her to flat-out rejection, but she never carried the pain for long. Instead, that hurt fueled her determination to make the next relationship succeed.

Enta always believed he could never do that—until he realized how much he wished Kazuki had caught him in the act of kissing him. Now he just felt utterly pathetic.

"Why the heck did I have to go and kiss him? Ugh!"

"I-It's closed!"

Kazuki was back at work searching for the lucky selfie item of the day. Decked out in his Sara outfit, he was currently standing in front of a specialty kisu fish store called Markiss's Riverside Fish Market. The owner of the store, Markiss Gimmemore, was said to be unrivaled in his ability to cut and handle kisu fish. A huge sign hung over his store with the slogan, "Eat a kisu and improve your ability to kiss-u too!"

Incidentally, there were rumors that the man was so incredibly handsome that he offered an additional service at his shop—women could take pictures with him as he hugged them from behind. He was basically an idol at this point, his business booming with female customers barging in daily.

"Sara's an idol, so I can't take a selfie of her kissing. I hoped I could take a joke selfie with a kisu since the name sounds similar, but... Now what am I going to do about today's mission?" For now, the only alternative he could think of was checking other fish markets around town.

Sara-Kazuki broke into a run, ignoring his skirt as it flapped up. Right now, he was only focused on one thing. He had to complete this mission—for Haruka.

Sarazanmai

PLATE 3

Kiss

SCENE 2

ENTA AND HARUKA sat on a bench by a pond, entertaining themselves with a game of Old Maid.

"Um, let's see...this one!" Haruka plucked one of the two cards Enta held out in his hand.

Left with only the joker, Enta shouted, "Argh, I lost again!"

"Lucky! I win!"

"You really are way too good at this, Haruka. I'm convinced Lady Luck is on your side."

"Ehehe, maybe that's thanks to Sara-chan?" His smartphone chimed. "Oh, a message!"

"From Kazuki?" asked Enta.

"It's a secret!"

There was a message in the chat window from Sara.

Sara: A plateful of apologies! It looks like today's lucky selfie is going to be a little late, dish!

Harukappa: Don't worry! Good luck!

The young boy quickly typed out his response before replying to Enta, "Kazu-chan and I don't message each other."

"I guess you do live together, so you can talk to each other as much as you want," Enta mused. Granted, the two were actually messaging each other all the time, albeit with Kazuki disguised as Sara, but Enta wasn't about to reveal that. But when he looked up, he noticed Haruka's face clouded over.

"He doesn't smile for me like he used to anymore," said the younger boy. "And he loved soccer so much, but he quit playing it. He even threw away his friendship bracelet."

"Yeah..." Enta, who was well aware of the situation, could say nothing in return. The friendship bracelet he stuffed inside his pocket felt heavier than ever.

"I actually really loved watching him play soccer," said Haruka.

"Me too. I loved playing with him more than anything."

"I'd like him to play again, but I'm not sure he'd listen to me. It's not up to me, anyway." Young as he was, Haruka really tried to be considerate about his older brother's feelings.

That just means I have to do what I can to help, Enta thought to himself.

"Don't worry! I'll have Kazuki smiling and playing soccer again! Trust me!" He stood and pounded a fist against his puffed-out chest.

"Ehehe! That's right, you two are the Golden Duo after all!"

"Yeah!"

A houseboat motored by as Otone stood next to the Sumida River, waiting in vain for her date.

She finally sighed and said, "Markiss sure is late. Normally he contacts me when he can't make it on time." She whipped out her phone and dialed his number.

Brrrrring...brrrrrrrring...

Back at Markiss's Riverside Fish Market, a smartphone lying on the floor began to vibrate, its owner nowhere to be seen. The screen read "Jinnai Otone," with a picture of Markiss hugging the girl in question from behind—until it was suddenly replaced by a bright red symbol of a heart, surrounded by static.

After parting ways with Haruka, Enta sat alone on the west side of the Azuma Bridge.

"So Kazuki doesn't even smile in front of Haruka anymore... not that it's any of my business," he mumbled self-deprecatingly.

Almost immediately, a voice shouted back, "It absolutely *is* your business!"

"Huh?" Enta glanced back to see Kazuki sprinting across the Azuma Bridge toward him. He was wearing his favorite windbreaker, the one he always wore for soccer. "Kazuki? What are you doing here?"

Kazuki stopped in front of him, an unusually serious expression on his face. "Enta, there's something I need to tell you."

"Wha...?" Enta's heart was about to jump out of his chest, with Kazuki gazing straight into his eyes. His intensity made Enta wonder if this was a love confession.

"I think I'm going to return to soccer."

"Huh?!"

Kazuki's proclamation was more astounding than any confession.

"Sorry to make you worry so much, Enta. I know I've put you through a lot, but will you join me in reforming our Golden Duo again?"

Enta's heart flooded with emotion. "Eep!" he squeaked. "You better not take this off again!" He adoringly tied the new friendship bracelet around Kazuki's ankle.

"I promise. We'll be the Golden Duo 'til death do us part."

"Kazukiii!"

For the first time in a very long time, the two of them did their signature pose.

"Dishing it out!" they shouted.

Ah, this is exactly what I've been wishing for, and at last it's become realit—

A voice cut through his reverie, dispelling the daydream. "Oh? You're going to give me this bracelet?"

"Huh?"

Kazuki had disappeared from his side and been replaced by Otone. She was wearing the bracelet around her ankle instead.

"S-sis?! Why are you here?!"

"I was on my way to go pick up my boyfriend. See ya!" She dashed off, leaving a dazed Enta behind.

"Wait! That's for Kazuki!" Enta returned to his senses and desperately scrambled after her. But when he made his way across the Azuma Bridge, he was greeted by an entirely different shocking sight.

"What are you guys doing?!" Enta flew down to his and Kazuki's secret training area.

Students from another school were there, practicing soccer. They turned and looked back when they heard his voice. "Hey, if it isn't Jinnai from Sara Junior High."

"Heya! What's up?" another called over to him.

Enta recognized the two. They were soccer players from a team he'd faced in competition last year. "This is our spot—mine and Kazuki's! You can't just use it without asking!"

"What the...? I have no idea what you're talking about."

"Kazuki, that's the other forward, right? I heard he quit soccer."

"Seriously? Then what's wrong with us using this spot?"

"Kazuki will be playing again soon!" swore Enta.

"You sure about that? He quit and left you hanging, didn't he? Kinda pathetic to get your hopes up over someone who ditched you like that."

"Shut up! I don't care what you say!" Contrary to what he said, he leaped on one of them and started throwing punches.

"Ouch!"

"Jerk, what are you doing?!" The other grabbed him by the collar of his shirt and shoved him away.

For Enta, who was quick to pick a fight in spite of being weak, the odds of winning a two-versus-one fight were practically zero.

"Graaaaaaah!"

That didn't stop Enta from charging toward them.

An imposing hush settled over the large conference room at the Asakusa Police Station, where a meeting was presently underway. A sign on the outside of the door read: *Asakusa Suspicious Death Investigation HQ.*

The chief's voice echoed inside the dimly lit room. "We identified the body we found early this morning as twenty-seven-year-old

Markiss Gimmemore, owner of the kisu specialty store Markiss's Riverside Fish Market. Six months ago, he entered into a relationship with a woman for the purpose of committing marriage fraud. When she committed suicide, we suspected that he drove her to it. However, we failed to bring charges against him, and he was released. We'll be investigating his death as a homicide."

There was an audible *ka-chik* as the projector flipped through photo after photo of Markiss cozying up to different women. Honestly, what was with all these cutesy romantic pictures anyway? To the gathered officers, Markiss's life looked more like a movie than reality. What did those girls see in this man? His face? Scam artist or not, being that popular was enough of a crime that he deserved to be behind bars. At least, that seemed to be the prevailing mood in the room.

Among those seated, two abruptly stood—Reo and Mabu.

"We're the ones who reeled him in!"

"It was yesterday's kiss!"

Yesterday evening, to be precise. The incident took place at the police box where the two worked.

"We've talked enough, haven't we?" Markiss asked. "I have to get up early tomorrow to go fishing with my honey."

"For those souls without beginnings or ends, those unable to connect..." Mabu held up a photo of Markiss out partying. A group of girls were hanging on his every word.

"Now, let us open a door..." Reo suddenly aimed the barrel of his gun at the man. "Is it desire?"

86

"Or love?"

A large taiko drum appeared above Markiss's head.

"Desire Extraction!"

In the next instant, Markiss was absorbed into the drum and disappeared completely.

Sarazanmai

PLATE 3

Kiss

SCENE 3

EVENING FELL on their practice spot. Enta was sprawled out on the ground. His face and body were covered in scratches, his training clothes ripped and torn.

"Whoa, hey, you jerks!"

"Ouch! Now you've done it!"

He could hear the faint sound of people quarreling. Someone else jumped in to fight in his place. Enta summoned the willpower to open his eyes. As he cracked them open, he spotted someone's right foot...with a friendship bracelet tied around their ankle.

"Kazuki...?"

The other students yelled bitterly at the interruption. "Don't get involved, this has nothing to do with you!"

After knocking one opponent to the ground, Kazuki stood protectively in front of Enta and said, "It absolutely does have something to do with me! Don't lay a hand on our Golden Duo!" Kazuki then landed a beautiful roundhouse kick on the boy that was still standing.

And with that, the fight was over.

"Enta, are you okay?"

Enta struggled to his feet, his voice heavy with frustration as he said, "Kazuki...don't put yourself in danger for my sake. If something happened to you, even death wouldn't bring me peace!"

Kazuki smoothly extended his hand toward Enta. "Don't worry. No matter what happens, we'll be the Golden Duo 'til death do us part."

The two of them immediately performed their signature pose. "Dishing it out!"

Ahh, I could die happy right now.

"Nah, you're not gonna die," a voice interrupted.

"Huh?"

Enta was still splayed out on the ground when he came to. Toi hovered above him, looking down. "K-Kuji?! Why are you here?!"

"You suck at fighting."

"Wh-where'd they go?! Don't tell me you chased them off?"

"Nah. I just asked what they were doing, and they took off running," said Toi as he began juggling the soccer ball they abandoned.

Enta could see the athletes from the other school in the distance, looking battered and worn-out as they ran off. "Damn it!"

"You know those guys?" Toi asked.

"They're from a team we beat last year."

"Aha."

Toi didn't express the slightest interest, but Enta continued anyway. Some of his wariness toward the other boy left him, perhaps because he'd just been utterly humiliated in front of Toi. "Our soccer team went pretty far in the competition, you know. Because...Kazuki was on our team last year. The day you transferred, Kazuki quit the team. But I still haven't accepted it."

"Not going to do you any good to obsess over someone who quit." Toi was completely right.

"Ever since we were kids, this is where we practiced. But now that Kazuki's gone, it doesn't have any meaning anymore."

After a pause, Toi said, "You guys are like brothers, then."

"Yeah, I guess. And I know if things keep going like this, Kazuki's never going to play soccer again."

"Then—"

"If I give up our spot, it's like accepting that it's over. I want to be a team again, to pass the ball to Kazuki again. That's why I need those Wishing Plates!"

Toi silently approached. Enta instinctively drew away as the other boy slipped past him. Then Toi glanced back and said, "I'm the one who's going to nab those plates. I'm not handing them over to either one of you."

It seemed that coming to an understanding with Toi would be impossible, after all. Enta focused on that instead of the guilt of not thanking Toi for helping him.

By the time the sun had set, Kazuki was out of his Sara outfit and sitting in the Kappa Plaza, pleading his case to Keppi.

"What am I going to do? There's no kisu anywhere. All the fish markets in the city are sold out."

"It's the work of the Kappa Zombies, ribbit," Keppi said, as if his answer were prerecorded. The plate on the top of his head spun around and lowered, revealing a mechanical arm that hoisted a TV into the air. A video of the Azuma Bridge was being streamed live on the screen. Since it was Keppi's device, Kazuki could plainly see the Kappa Zombie, despite remaining in his human form.

In the middle of the bridge was a Kappa Zombie with the head of a kisu. Women lined up in front of it, each wearing a bridal gown. As they came up to plant a kiss on his lips, they too were turned into fish. He spotted a familiar figure among those girls still waiting for their turn—Otone!

"Sis?!" Enta exclaimed, rushing up in time to catch a glimpse of her. Toi followed just a few steps behind him.

On the monitor, Otone wore Enta's friendship bracelet tightly around her ankle.

That was supposed to be for Kazuki, Enta thought as he demanded, "Keppi! Turn us into kappa!" He leaped forward without thinking.

"Desiiiire...Extractioooon!!"

Keppi slammed into Enta's proffered butt.

"The object of this Kappa Zombie's desire is kisses, ribbit."

A little embarrassed by the word and its implications, Toi bashfully commented, "Well, my brother did say KISS is the devil."

"It doesn't matter, I need a kisu for Haruka!"

"And I need to get that friendship bracelet back!"

With a fire lit in all of their hearts, the curtain opened on the night's battle.

"Kappature it!" Keppi cried as the three of them flew toward the creature.

"Quantity over quality! All that matters is *how many* kisses I've stolen!" said the zombie.

Disgusted, Enta replied, "You value the number of kisses over the quality?"

"I want to be loved by all the women of the world!"

"What the heck is this guy going on about?" Enta's anger rose as he listened to the zombie's assertions. "Kissing has no point if you do it with anyone! A kiss is how you express a love for someone that's too strong to contain anymore!" With Kappa-Enta's cry, the Kappa Zombie's body began to fracture.

"Saraaa!"

"Saraaa!"

"Saraaa!"

And then all together, "Sarazanmai!"

As the transfer of the zombie's shirikodama began, Enta realized for the first time just what he'd done. Plucking out the marble of energy meant that it would be his secret revealed next. It was too late to regret his actions now. Enta trembled with fear, anticipating what was to come as his vision blurred and transformed.

"Leaking."

The first scene they witnessed was of the soccer team's locker room. Enta snuck away during one of their breaks and was now standing in front of a locker with "Yasaka" written on the nameplate. Enta swiftly swung the door open and grabbed for Kazuki's training clothes. He squeezed them against his chest and breathed out, pushing all the air out of his lungs. Then he buried his face in the fabric, drawing in the smell.

"Stop! Don't waaaaatch!!"

He didn't want this. Yes, he had wanted Kazuki to know how he felt, but this went above and beyond confessing his love to Kazuki. This was the *one thing* that he absolutely wanted to take to his grave!

Toi took the shirikodama from Enta. As he drifted in the seas of their shared consciousness, he felt conflicted. Was it appropriate for him to see whatever was about to be shown to him? But once begun, the "leak" couldn't be stopped, and their consciousnesses began to combine.

The next scene was of a classroom, bathed in the light of a sunset. Once again, Enta ducked away from the soccer club to go rifling through Kazuki's desk. What he pulled out was a recorder case. It was easy to imagine where this was going to lead.

Even though Toi wasn't the one getting exposed by this leak, he still found himself wanting to scream, *No more!*

In the red glow of the classroom stood Enta, gripping Kazuki's recorder in his hands. He stared unblinkingly at the tip before resolutely popping his mouth over it. Toi could feel the pleasure— the satisfaction that Enta felt at this almost-kiss—as if it were Toi's own, though he wished he didn't.

"You've got to be kidding me..." he muttered.

The shirikodama shifted from Toi's hands to Kazuki's, and at last, the final scene began to play. It was from the night before, by the riverbank, when Enta planted a kiss on the sleeping Sara-Kazuki.

"Enta...kissed me?"

Since they were linked, Enta could feel Kazuki's confusion directly. It was all he could do to scream, "It's all oooooooooover!"

As the Desire Field over the Azuma Bridge dissipated, Otone regained consciousness.

"Where am I...?"

Despite the late hour, there were many other women walking around on the bridge. Otone saw her fishing equipment by her side and remembered the date she had planned.

"That's right! I was supposed to meet up with him!" Panicked, she pulled out her cellphone, intending to apologize for being late, but then... "Huh? Hold on, who was I waiting for?"

In the image on her phone's home screen, she now stood alone. The man who had been hugging her from behind disappeared from the picture.

Elsewhere in the city, Reo was riding on an underground elevator, a picture in his hand, as the image of Markiss slowly faded from the frame. "Humans sure are foolish. Their ties to one another are so fragile, but they cling to them anyway."

Mabu listened quietly as a robotic voice announced, "Call incoming from the Empire. Call incoming from the Empire."

The two immediately took a knee as they faced a pillar with a heart symbol on it.

"How otterly strange. There's been a sharp decline in the amount of Desire Energy you've been sending us lately. I don't doubt your loyalty, but I must remind you that betraying the Empire means death."

Mabu kept his expression obedient and regretful as he replied, "Our most humble apologies. Meddlers have appeared."

"Otterly unbelievable. I don't want to hear your excuses. Endeavor to provide more."

"As you say," Reo replied with superficial courtesy, and the transmission ended.

PLATE 3

Kiss

SCENE 4

"**U**NFORTUNATELY, today's Wishing Plate is silver once again, ribbit."

Enta accepted the dish, a cold sweat beading on his skin.

"Hey, Enta," Kazuki called over, "about that kiss..."

"Huh?! U-uh, about that...!"

As Enta scrambled desperately to form a coherent reply, Toi stood in the background, looking like he wanted to be anywhere but here. Considering the price Enta paid for their victory, he didn't even entertain the idea of stealing the plate from him.

Kazuki, on the other hand, seemed completely indifferent. "I'm not really bothered by it. I'm guessing you lost a bet with someone on the team, right? That's why you did all those things? It's got nothing to do with me since I'm not on the team anymore anyway."

Those words triggered something in Enta. "It absolutely *does* have something to do with you!" Once the words had been spoken, they couldn't be taken back. Enta felt his stomach tie itself in knots. "You're all I think about. I know the reason that you quit the soccer club and stopped smiling isn't something I can fix. But the two of us playing soccer together meant everything to me! That's why I thought it was my turn to finally... Aw, shoot!"

If he said any more, he might burst into tears. Enta decided to stop resisting and just get it over with. He put the friendship bracelet on top of the silver plate and held it out toward the other boy. "I love you! Be my partner—be a part of the Golden Duo with me for life!" He bent his head down, but he could still hear Kazuki gulp.

Finally, it'll all be over. I can cut off my feelings and be rid of them once and for all...!

Kazuki reached out his hand and gently took the plate from him. "I understand how you feel now."

Enta lifted his chin, shocked to find Kazuki smiling as he only ever did in Enta's dreams.

"We'll be the Golden Duo 'til death do us part."

"K-Kazuki...!"

Kazuki inched forward toward Enta, the new friendship bracelet now tied around his foot. Enta mirrored his movement and took a step closer as well. Everything around them seemed to fade away, as if a spotlight had fallen on just the two of them. Kazuki reached out and placed a hand on Enta's shoulder, gripping it tightly. Enta softly closed his eyes, lifting himself up on the balls of his feet to get closer. Their lips inched closer, closer—

"Kiss, kiss, ribbit~! ♡"

His eyes flew open to the sight of Keppi's face. It was so close it was swallowing up his vision.

"Mmmwaah! I stole your kiss, ribbit!"

"Agh! Gyehhh!" Enta ran from the blushing Keppi and began emptying the contents of his stomach onto the ground.

Toi, who watched the whole thing from beginning to end, wore an expression on his face that almost seemed to say, *See? I told you that KISS is the devil.*

"Enta? What's wrong?" The *real* Kazuki was preoccupied with writing a message to Haruka and completely missed the whole thing.

"Huh?! Uh, er, it's nothing!" *I knew it,* Enta thought. *I knew it was just another one of my delusions!*

"Your clothes are all torn up too," Kazuki noticed. "Did something happen?"

"Huh? Oh, this? I just took a bad fall, that's all!"

"You really are a klutz, aren't you, Enta?"

"Yeah, I sure am! Aha, ha ha ha!" he exclaimed with a dry laugh. Kazuki's indifference both saved him and brought him crashing back down to reality countless times before. This time was no exception, and Enta elected to take advantage of his friend's obliviousness to drop the matter.

Toi stared at Enta's face and noticed something. Out of nowhere, a rat appeared on top of the silver plate Enta was holding.

"Meep, meep, meep!" It chomped down on the friendship bracelet and scurried away at a blinding speed, jetting into one of the drainage ducts that lined the streets.

A few seconds too late, Enta pathetically shouted into the duct after the little thief. "Wait! Aaah!!"

Sarazanmai

PLATE 3

Kiss

SCENE 5

A S HARUKA SAT on a bench waiting, Enta approached.

It was a Sunday. Normally, Enta would do his morning practice at their secret spot before going to meet Haruka. This time, however, he had a glum look on his face. He plopped down on the bench and spat out, "Ugh, it's no use. It's pointless! Nothing I say seems to reach Kazuki at all."

Haruka watched anxiously as the older boy raged on. "I mean, I've always known that, I just pretended I didn't. But now I feel like a sumo wrestler doing a match all by myself—pathetic!" Enta lifted himself back to his feet, raising his arms up in the air as if he were about to stretch, the expression on his face no longer visible to Haruka. "I give up. I can't do this. I'm not going to bother trying to get him back, and I'm not going to expect anything from him—"

"Enta?"

"Hm?" Enta glanced back to find Haruka holding his palm out toward him. Resting in the boy's tiny hand was a slightly worn-out friendship bracelet.

"That bracelet..."

SARAZANMAI

"I snuck it out of the trash. It's the one Kazu-chan tried to throw away." Haruka reached out and tucked the friendship bracelet into Enta's hand. "I can't keep up with him anymore, so... would you be the one to return it to him someday?"

"Huh, wait, no! I don't have..." *The right to*, he intended to say, but he hesitated as he dropped himself back onto the bench. His feelings for Kazuki hadn't changed; they were strong and impossible to get rid of. But Enta just proclaimed he was giving up his position as Kazuki's best friend, and it made him anxious to consider accepting this bracelet and everything that went along with it.

"Everything will be okay!" Haruka said with a grin. "You two are the Golden Duo, right?"

Ever since Kazuki rejected him using those same words, Enta had been waiting for someone to say that to him. He closed his fist tight around the bracelet. *Is it really okay for me to keep trying?* he wondered. *No, there's no way I could ever really give up. After all, we are the Golden Duo!*

"Thanks, Haruka!"

"Ehehe!"

As the two of them smiled at each other, a voice called in the distance. "Haruka! It's time to come in!" They looked up to see Haruka's mother waving her hand.

"Okay!" Enta called back energetically, lifting himself back off the bench.

"I had a really good dream today," said Haruka.

"Really?" Enta asked as he unfolded the wheelchair propped up behind the bench. He helped Haruka settle onto it.

"Thanks for always doing this, Enta-kun," said the boy's mother.

Ever since Haruka lost his ability to walk, Enta unfailingly showed up every Sunday to accompany him to physical therapy.

"It's my pleasure," Enta replied to her before turning back to Haruka. "So, what kind of dream was it?"

"I hopped onto a huge Nyantaro and rode her all the way out to space. Then I met the prince of the stars!"

"Ha ha ha, what kind of dream is that?!"

And so that Sunday afternoon went by quietly like all the others before it.

Rain

THE RAIN OF LIFE pours ceaselessly.

In this country, rain is treated like a gift from the heavens. Rain invigorates the land, breathes life into plants and animals. All living things need it, no matter how big or small.

When I was little, I hated rainy days. Rain seemed to sharpen the loneliness in my life, its cold, icy claws gripping my heart tight as I searched futilely for shelter. I would rather die than beg the heavens for relief. I didn't believe in God. Honestly, this world could have dried up for all I cared.

To my annoyance, it was raining that day, too—the day he reached out to me. I looked at his pristine, unblemished hands, and I felt ashamed of the filth that covered my own. And yet, at the same time, I found myself wanting to soil his hands so they were like mine. In the shadowed corners of my lifeless heart, a small ember of desire came alive.

"Don't let go of that. Desire is what keeps you alive."

All I wanted was somewhere to belong, a voice to answer my calls—for some warmth to caress my outstretched hand. That was what I needed, not rain.

You were the one who helped me realize that.

Rainy days reminded him of things he'd rather not remember. Reo sat lost in reverie, glaring out the window with a bitter look on his face. The sky had been threatening rain all day in Asakusa.

Mabu was out, and Reo had a pretty good idea where his partner had gone. His suspicions only worsened his mood.

"Hurry up and come home, Mabu."

The words—his true feelings—fell from his lips like droplets of water. Even though he was an adult now, he still hated the rain. It made him remember the feeling of his outstretched hand as his fingertips brushed against a stone-cold heart.

PLATE 4

Soba

SCENE 1

THE MEMORY still haunted Toi's dreams. The memory of a winter four years ago, before he left Asakusa. The hollow sound of a gun firing, a flash of light, then the cloying stench of gunpowder and the vibrant color red. The air was bone-chillingly frigid outside, and yet the thing in his hand felt even colder.

"In this world, it's only the bad people who survive."

The expression on his older brother's face was seared into Toi's mind, unforgettable.

Sarazanmai

PLATE 4

Soba

SCENE 2

"**G**OOD MORNING! ☆ Every day is happy! And with your lucky selfie, you'll have even more happiness on your plate! It's me, Azuma Sara, dish! ☆" Sara's dreamy voice came drifting out of the living room TV.

"Good morning! ☆ It's me, Harukappa, dish!" Haruka called back, waving to the TV.

"Tomorrow is finally the day, Haruka," called his mother.

"Yeah!"

"Enta-kun is coming as well, isn't he?" asked the boy's father.

"That's right! I can't wait!" Haruka's cheerful voice echoed throughout the Yasaka home.

After a deep breath, Kazuki slid the living room door open. He was immediately greeted by Haruka's smile as the boy sat atop his wheelchair.

"Kazu-chan, morning!"

Their father, a designer, had renovated every corner of their house with keen attention to detail. All the steps that might impede a wheelchair were removed, and the toilet and bath areas were widened. He installed new doors that slid aside rather than swung open. Handrails decorated the walls across the house, so that Haruka could eventually use them for balance once he was able to get back on his feet again.

Kazuki turned his eyes away from all of that as he stood there, waiting.

It was routine for Haruka's father to accompany his younger son to the promenade and then back home again so Haruka could feed Nyantaro. And, like always, he took a seat on the terrace of a nearby coffee shop, sipping his drink while he waited for Haruka to finish. Kazuki knew that this was his father's way of giving his sons some space to talk... but he never knew how to take advantage of it. He slumped back against the embankment wall, smartphone in hand as he checked on today's lucky selfie horoscope.

"Now then, what will today's lucky selfie item be?" On the screen, Sara stopped the spinning roulette wheel and said, *"So-bang! It's soba, dish! ☆"*

"Soba, huh..." Kazuki mumbled to himself. Fortunately, there was no shortage of soba restaurants in Asakusa. Instant cup soba could just as easily work, too.

Just as Kazuki was making these plans, an incredible piece of news suddenly drifted to his ears.

"And finally, an important announcement! Tomorrow in Asakusa, I'll be at a meet-and-greet event, dish! ☆ That's right, you'll be able to shake my hand, dish! ☆ I hope you'll all come to see me~! ☆"

"What?!" Kazuki shrieked.

"Hey, Kazu-chan, this means tomorrow I'll be able to meet Sara-chan!" said Haruka. "Isn't that amazing?"

"Wait, don't tell me...you mean the handshake event?"

"That's right! I'm kind of nervous since it'll be my first time meeting her in real life!"

Sara droned on from his phone, *"Okay then, have a wonderful day, and may lots of luck be dished your way!"*

If you took Asakusa's Orange Street into the Tanuki Shopping District, one of the first places you'd see was a soba restaurant called Sobakyuu. The place had a solid reputation, with regulars constantly bustling in and out. Despite that, few people remembered the old store before its current ownership took over.

Toi currently lay in the apartment above the restaurant, on the phone with his brother. It was a tatami room, six straw mats in size. Cardboard boxes were stacked around the room and left sealed, the same way they'd been since Toi's return.

Toi could hear both his brother's voice and the slosh of water through the receiver. He didn't need to ask to know what his brother was doing. Not after all these years.

"Yeah, nothing much to report on my end," he said. "How about you?"

"Same old, same old," answered Chikai. "Nothing for you to worry about."

"Okay..."

"How's your new school? Made some friends?"

"I don't need friends. We're going to blow this place eventually anyway," said Toi.

"C'mon, don't say that. How's our aunt and uncle? They're looking after you, right?"

Toi huffed. "Who cares about them?"

"Are they saying nasty things to you because of me? Sorry 'bout that."

"I don't care what they say to me! You're the one who protected this store, so how can they—"

"It's fine," Chikai said, cutting him off. "That's between you and me. A secret we're gonna keep for life."

"I know. You protected this place, so that's why I decided I'd wait here for you."

As he lay on his back, surrounded by the thick smell of tatami, Toi twirled the gun in his hand. The same gun that upended his older brother's life just four years ago. To Toi, the gun felt like the embodiment of a curse. He kept it with him all the time. That way, even if the two of them were apart, he could still feel like they were connected, like he shared the weight of his brother's sins. The weight of it kept him grounded, the mercilessly cold steel of it a reminder that he would never be forgiven for what he'd done.

"I've got good news. I should be able to drop by and see you soon," said Chikai.

Toi launched himself up off the floor. "Seriously?! So, I can go with you next time, then?!"

"Hmm, I don't know, can you?"

"We promised, right? That once everything was settled, the two of us would live together. I don't want to be apart anymore."

"I feel the same way, you know. I feel *so bad* that I couldn't be with you more."

A knock sounded, and Toi slipped his gun in behind his belt. He knew they would never open the door, but it never hurt to be careful. The frightened voice of his aunt drifted in through the thin paper of the sliding door. "Toi-chan? A boy is here to see you, says he's your friend."

A friend?

He had no clue who that could be... Okay, no, he *did* know who it could be, he just loathed trouble.

Toi walked down the steps in a foul mood. When he got to the bottom, he locked eyes with his uncle, who was busy prepping for the restaurant's opening. He deliberately averted his gaze and headed out the front door.

His aunt's worried voice chased after him. "You stay out so late every night, where are you going? You're not doing anything dangerous, are you?"

"Not like he's going to listen to you! He's too stubborn to cut ties with that murdering bastard of a brother, after all!" For better or worse, Toi's uncle was an honest man, and he didn't mince words.

Toi didn't want to listen to their jabbering any further, so he slammed the door shut behind him. The name of this place hadn't changed, but everything else had, ever since the incident. The flavor of the soba, Chikai, and even Toi himself.

"So it's *you*..." He suspected as much, but it irked him to be right.

"J-just so we're clear, I only lied and said we were friends so I could call you out here, okay?!" Enta stood in front of him, still clad in his practice uniform.

"Yeah, whatever."

Enta considerately led them away from his family's restaurant and to an empty lot to talk, but he had no compunction about broaching the very topic Toi would have rather left untouched. "Oh, and I didn't know your family ran a soba restaurant! My family eats Sobakyuu for New Year's every year. The soba at your place is really good!" Enta made a big display of bouncing his soccer ball around, juggling it with his feet as he spoke.

It left Toi dumbfounded. "Glad to hear it," he said dryly.

"But you transferred to our school from somewhere else, right? How come?"

Toi sighed and stared up at the sky as he slowly began to explain. It wasn't because Enta had complimented the restaurant, or anything—his mood had just softened, and he wasn't bristling anymore. "After my mom and dad passed away, we left Asakusa for a while. My relatives inherited the store. I just live there."

"Oh, okay...sorry," Enta said, apologizing sincerely.

Toi changed the subject. "Anyway, what'd you come to me for?"

"Oh yeah! That's right!" Enta dropped the soccer ball and bowed his head down in front of Toi. "I'm begging you! Please give your Wishing Plate to Kazuki!"

He suspected as much. This was the only reason Enta would bother approaching him, after all. "I don't... He's put you through the wringer and caused you nothing but pain. How are you not fed up with him?"

From Toi's perspective, Kazuki's indifference toward Enta couldn't be so easily forgiven. Especially since the other boy's feelings bled into Toi's consciousness, and he was now keenly aware of just how Enta felt. It was also obvious that Kazuki had no room in his heart for anyone but his little brother.

"Kazuki saved me from a life of loneliness. And I've decided that it's my turn to help him this time!"

Those words jolted Toi's memory.

His brother had told him long ago, "In this world, those who can't survive have to disappear." And those who disappeared were forgotten. That went for people as well as towns, buildings— everything. Once something disappeared, it was overwritten by something new, like data. And in this city, no one stopped to notice. Asakusa was a city prone to sudden, extreme change. Tourist spots that couldn't cut it were left struggling to outlast each other.

With the city as a backdrop, he found himself wandering to the seaside water bus stop where he'd last seen his brother.

"'It's my turn to help him,' huh...?"

It pained him to admit it, but Enta's words and feelings tugged at his heartstrings. Both Enta and Kazuki were trouble, but Enta in a different way than the latter.

That thought seemed to summon the other troublesome person in question—Kazuki—who appeared decked out in his Sara outfit.

"There you are! Kuuuuji!" Sara-Kazuki came blasting full speed down the promenade toward him. The other boy didn't even slow as he approached, but instead, threw his arms around Toi.

"Guh?!"

He could hear Kazuki's voice ringing in his ears. "Help me kidnap Azuma Sara! Dish! ☆"

"What?!"

With that, Toi found himself caught up in what would most definitely turn out to be *immense* trouble.

"Phoo, phoo..."

Sara-Kazuki had purchased some instant cup soba from the convenience store and was now sitting in the high-rise parking lot, blowing on his noodles to cool them. His lightly colored lips were puckered adorably as he did so.

Pa-chik.

Toi captured the image on his smartphone before mumbling in exasperation, "Okay, you've gotta be kidding, right?"

"Ehehe, I am being completely serious, dish! ☆" Sara-Kazuki tilted his head back slightly and smiled.

The memory of their first meeting flashed through Toi's mind. He'd been in the middle of trying to break into a car when Kazuki, dressed as Azuma Sara, happened upon him. At the time, he honestly thought that Kazuki looked cute.

"Tomorrow—*shlurp, shlurp*—before the handshake event, I'd like you to—*shlurp, shlurp*—kidnap her—*shlurp, shlurp*..." He was noisily slurping up his noodles, as was custom, yet the fanfare seemed ridiculous considering he was eating only one noodle at a time.

"You really suck at eating noodles," observed Toi.

Gulp...gulp... As Sara-Kazuki tilted the bowl back to drink the dashi broth, the light in the background framed his silhouette like a painting.

Ba-thump, ba-thump.

Toi found the thrumming of his heart annoyingly loud.

"Pwaaah! You're the only person I can entrust with such a request, Kuji."

He felt slightly disappointed watching Kazuki return to his normal self after looking so cute, but Toi dismissed the thought, trying to keep his cool, aloof air. "If you get found out, you know it'll be serious trouble."

"Don't worry, I'll be taking her place. I promised Haruka I would use our secret code when we shake hands."

"Gimme a break," said Toi. "You know there's no way this is gonna go well."

"I've kept this secret all this time! And I have to keep up the charade that *I'm* Sara, for Haruka's sake!"

Toi was at a loss against Sara-Kazuki's impassioned pleas. Once again, his thoughts were sent reeling back to the past.

The weak have to be protected in order to survive. That was a lesson he learned early.

A flier had been posted on Sobakyuu's door. *Dear customers,* it read. *Due to the untimely death of the owners, the store will be closing.*

In the winter when he was ten, Toi's parents passed away. Later, he pieced together that his parents had been saddled with an enormous debt after being conned by one of their friends. Chikai was already hanging out with the wrong crowd back then and rarely came home. Even so, the young Toi had no one else to rely on except his older brother.

Time went by in a daze as he gazed at the urns where his parents' ashes were kept, and at their portrait. Both sat on a floor desk beside him. Even when day turned to dusk, he couldn't even bother to flip on the lights.

One day, a sudden, violent thumping came up the stairs, and Toi's entire body tensed. The door rattled as it was thrust open, revealing Chikai wearing an embroidered baseball jacket.

"Brother..." Toi mumbled, but before he could welcome his older sibling home, he heard something light and round bounce off the floor and come rolling to a stop at his feet. It was a ten-thousand-yen bill that Chikai balled up and tossed at him.

"There. Use that and figure out how to feed yourself." Chikai began rifling through his parents' chest of drawers, grinning as he produced a pearl necklace.

"That's Mom's," Toi said reproachfully.

Chikai, whose mood had taken a dark, vicious turn, spat back, "Once you're dead, it's all over. If it means we can get some cash, I'm sure that's what those two would've wanted."

The way Chikai referred to their parents as if they were strangers—"those two"—seemed to open up a chasm between them.

"Dad always said not to do bad things," Toi protested.

That didn't stop Chikai from continuing to rummage around for any other valuables. "Yeah, like an idiot, he pretended to be some kinda saint and look where it got him."

Toi couldn't hold back his anger anymore. "I hate you for saying such horrible things about Mom and Dad! It should've been you instead of them!"

Thwump! In the blink of an eye, his brother was upon him, grabbing him by the jaw and shoving him roughly up against the wall.

"Hrgh!" Tears sprang to his eyes, both from fear and the pain.

"I'll run you through...!" Chikai threatened, then calmed himself down enough to say, "Listen up, Toi. In this world, it's only the bad people who survive."

On a different evening, he watched through a window as his brother met up with someone in the alley behind Sobakyuu. The man was muscular, with a fierce look on his face. Toi had no way of knowing at the time, but this man was Yuri Kamome, the young leader of a powerful group in Asakusa called YURIKAMOME.

Kamome tried handing a cloth-wrapped object to Chikai.

"Chikai, you're an adult now. You can handle somethin' like this," he giggled.

"No, I'm not ready for that yet," replied Chikai.

"Then how about this. I'm leaving this in your hands for safekeeping, as an older brother to a younger brother. You won't refuse me then, will ya?"

Chikai sensed that refusing the man any further would be a bad idea. He let out a quiet sigh and said, "All right," as he took the object.

Kamome's laughter echoed eerily down the dark street.

Toi crawled into bed and pretended to sleep. It wasn't long before Chikai came into the room. The floor desk rattled as he slid one of the drawers open, but just as quickly he headed back out again. Once he was gone, Toi slipped out of bed and timidly checked the drawer. Tucked inside, gleaming silver in the dark, was a Tokarev gun.

"...My brother really is a bad person."

In front of their parents' portrait, Chikai had casually left another wrinkled ten-thousand-yen bill.

Soon enough, Sobakyuu was forced to close its doors.

"Are we going to be thrown out? Are we going to lose Mom and Dad's restaurant?" Toi asked his brother, who'd returned home for the first time in a long time.

But his brother only replied coldly, "Those who can't survive have to disappear. Disappear and be left behind, forgotten."

"I don't want that! I don't want to forget them! Not our parents, and not the taste of our soba, either...!" Toi vehemently opposed the idea, though there was nothing a powerless child like him could do about it.

The day before they were to be evicted, his aunt and uncle came to clean up the store.

"Stop it! Don't touch our restaurant!"

As Toi clung to his uncle's legs, the older man stared down at him as if he were some kind of bug. "You can complain all you like, they're still going to evict you tomorrow."

"It really is a shame this place has to close down," said his wife.

"That's how it goes if you can't pay. You and your brother should just be glad that we're looking after you."

It really is over, Toi thought, about to give up. But then—

"If it's money you need, I got it." Chikai pushed the door open and stood at the entrance.

"Chikai! Where have you been all this time?"

Chikai ignored his uncle's question and slammed an attaché case down on a nearby table. It was lined with stacks of cash and, in the center, the deed to the restaurant. "I got the restaurant back, and I'm giving you this cash. So..." He turned to his aunt and uncle, who were struck speechless at seeing such a huge sum of money for the first time in their lives. "Please, take over the place."

It was a bitter decision for the two brothers to have to make.

Toi understood now how powerless he'd been, and that he was nothing but a burden for his brother to protect.

"Kuji? You listening?" Sara-Kazuki called out to him, disrupting the pool of memories he submerged himself in.

"Huh? Oh, my bad," said Toi.

Sara-Kazuki was bent down on the ground, a blueprint spread out beneath him. He moved chips across it, ones with portraits drawn on their sides. "You following me? The day of the event, Sara will enter this waiting room. First, you need to lock her manager in this bathroom. After that, you can call Sara out of the room, and I'll use that opportunity to sneak in." He nodded to himself. "Yeah, this plan is perfect, dish! ☆"

"Hold on a second."

"Hm?"

"How come *I'm* the one doing everything?" Toi complained.

"I told you, you're the only person I can trust with this! I have to concentrate on passing myself off as Sara, disssrgh...!"

Sara-Kazuki's voice turned into muffled groans as Toi squeezed the boy's face in his hand. Kazuki dropped his cup of soba, and it went plummeting downward before coming to a soft stop a few inches above the ground, where it began to float upward.

"My soba!" Kazuki gasped.

"A Kappa Zombie!"

An imposing hush settled over the large conference room at the Asakusa Police Station, where a meeting was presently under-way. A paper on the outside of the door read: *Asakusa Suspicious Death Investigation HQ.*

The chief's voice echoed inside the dimly lit room. "We have identified the body we found early this morning: thirty-year-old Sobatani Yudeo." His profile revealed that his name included the kanji for "boiling hot soba boy." "He's the owner of the restaurant Soba no Yu. Six months ago, he was arrested on suspicion of sneaking into the home of one of his female customers and stealing her used bathwater. He was released after we failed to bring charges against him. We'll be investigating his death as a homicide."

There was an audible *ka-chik* as the projector flipped through the images, eventually landing on a photo of the crime scene. Hoses crawled down from the window of the victim's bathroom, pumping into plastic containers where the criminal stored the stolen bathwater.

The prevailing mood of the room was, *Damn, this guy's seriously creepy, isn't he?*

"We're the ones who sucked him up!" said Reo.

"It was yesterday's soba!" said Mabu.

Yesterday evening, to be precise. The incident took place at the police box where the two worked.

"Well, I have to prep for opening tomorrow, so..."

"For those souls without beginnings or ends, those unable to connect..." Mabu held up a photo of Sobatani threading the hoses through the woman's bathroom window, plastic containers in his hands.

"Now, let us open a door..." Reo aimed the barrel of his gun at the man. "Is it desire?"

"Or love?"

A large taiko drum appeared above Sobatani's head.

"Desire Extraction!"

Sobatani was sucked into the drum and disappeared completely.

The Desire Field wrapped itself around the entire area of Asakusa, and the Zombie's underlings began swiping all of the soba throughout the city. Sobakyuu was no exception.

"Oh no! Our soba...!" Toi's uncle watched as their bowls of noodles went flying away, one after another. Helpless to stop them, he collapsed to his knees.

Toi watched the scene unfold on Keppi's monitor.

Enta gasped from beside him, "Wait, that's Sobakyuu, isn't it?!"

"Tch," Toi clicked his tongue. He grabbed Keppi by the beak and threateningly hissed, "Turn me into a kappa right now!"

"Ribbit?!"

Toi turned his back to Keppi, and the Crown Prince of Kappa slammed into him from behind.

"Desiiiire Extractiooon!"

"The object of this Kappa Zombie's desire is soba, ribbit."

"Kuji, is your restaurant going to be okay?" asked Kappa-Enta.

"Huh? Kuji's family runs a soba restaurant?" Kappa-Kazuki's eyes widened. It was the first he heard of this.

"If someone steals from you, you take back what's yours!"

"Kappature it!" Keppi cried as the three of them flew toward the creature.

"I love the girl who likes my soba!" The Kappa Zombie mercilessly threw bowls of soba at the boys. "Leftover bathwater isn't enough! I want to be with her *so bad*!"

Kappa-Toi gave the creature's whining a direct, verbal smackdown. "You're just forcing your selfishness on other people! If you really 'want to be with her *so bad*', then man up!"

"Gyaaaaaaah!"

Kappa-Toi dove into the creature's rectum and grasped its shirikodama in his hands. He desperately cried, "I want to protect the same thing my brother fought to protect!"

"We kappatured it!" the three declared.

As he held the ball of energy in his hand, Kappa-Toi saw the man's desire—him and the girl soaking in a bath filled with soba water, her eating noodles soaked in broth made from her leftover bathwater.

"I found the perfect dashi..." said the man in his fantasy.

"So that's it," Kappa-Toi realized. "You wanted to use the bathwater you stole to boil soba..."

"My secret's been found ooooooout!"

Sobatani's Kappa Zombie body began to fracture.

"Saraaa!"

"Saraaa!"

"Saraaa!"

And then all together, "Sarazanmai!"

As the transfer of the shirikodama began, Toi felt something akin to resignation. That emotion was soon transferred to the other two as well.

"Leaking."

They saw a scene from a winter day four years ago. It was right after Chikai disappeared after saving Sobakyuu.

Toi's breath puffed out in white clouds as he ran through Asakusa. "Brother, where did you go? Don't leave me behind!" As he passed by one alleyway, he heard a familiar laugh.

"Ehehehe..."

He stilled his breathing and peered out from the shadows, spotting Yuri Kamome and his underling, Yasuda Yasu.

"Kwaaah! Chikai, that bastard. Looks like he hasn't gone back home yet. And the old man workin' there says he cut ties with Chikai, so he doesn't know nothin'," said Yasu.

"Ah, well. It's just a matter of time before he slips up. He's barkin' up the wrong tree if he thinks he can defy us, steal from us, and get away. Ehehehe." Kamome's eyes peeled wide open as he laughed. "If you find him, shoot him. He's got my gun."

"Kwaaah!"

Having heard their conversation, Toi hastened back home.

Now that Sobakyuu had reopened, customers were gradually beginning to return. When Toi pressed the door open and entered, his uncle immediately scolded him. "Toi! I told you to enter from the back!"

Without stopping to reply, Toi scrambled up the stairs to the second floor. Inside the room, a single thousand-yen bill sat in front of his parents' portrait. It hadn't been there this morning. When he yanked the drawer to the desk open, he found the gun still remained, its presence as oppressive as ever.

So, his brother wasn't walking around with the gun on him. As he went to shut the drawer again, a slip of paper tucked beneath the gun caught his eye. He pulled it out and flipped it over. It was a photo of him and Chikai when they were younger, smiling. One they'd taken together as a family when Toi was five.

Warm memories filled him, one after the other. Making and eating soba together as a family. Him and Chikai standing out in front of the store during Sanja Festival, wearing happi coats and selling soba. The two of them walking to a flower garden together on one of their rare days off.

"Brother...!"

I knew this was going to happen...! Toi was prepared for his memories to leak. But when he thought about how that meant reexperiencing *that day* all over again, he couldn't help but feel like he was somehow betraying his brother. This was supposed to be a secret between the two of them, forever.

The shirikodama transferred to Kazuki.

YURIKAMOME, frustrated by being unable to locate Chikai, had set its sights on his younger brother instead. Toi, however, couldn't risk being a burden to Chikai by letting them capture him. He ran with everything he had.

Above him, on the Azuma Bridge, men in the same embroidered baseball jackets he'd seen his brother wear were talking about him.

"That little brat... Where the heck is he hiding?!"

"We need him as a hostage to lure Chikai out! We *have* to find him!"

"Kwaaah!"

When their footsteps began to fade, Toi chanced a peek out from the tunnel where he was hiding, its entrance lined by stones. He had to hurry. But where? Where could he go? His footsteps felt heavy as he wandered down the tunnel.

"Hey, kiddo, where you goin'?"

Toi's head jerked up to find Yuri Kamome standing ahead of him at the exit.

"Ehehehe. How about I tag along with you?"

One step, then two. Kamome was making his way closer.

Unable to stand it anymore, Kazuki cried out, "Run!"

Having received the shirikodama from Kazuki, Enta shared in his friend's terror. But it was the eerie calm that settled over Toi in the vision that worried him.

Bang!

For a split second, the inside of that tunnel lit up like a sunny day. A lead bullet buried itself in Kamome's stomach, and his hulking form sank to the ground. The scene played out in slow motion for Toi.

He was breathing as hard as if he'd just run a sprint. He

belatedly realized his hands were trembling as they clasped the grip of the pistol.

He'd taken a life. With this gun.

Behind the fallen Yuri Kamome was a silhouette he knew all too well.

"Bro..."

He had been searching so desperately for his older brother, and now he felt like running away.

This was awful. Scary. He was a *murderer*.

Help! I'm sorry. Dad, Mom...!

Chikai walked straight toward him.

Toi's legs refused to budge, as if his feet were sewn to the ground. He snapped his eyes shut and felt something icy brush against his hands. It was Chikai's hand. With a soft touch, his brother peeled Toi's trembling fingers back and lifted the gun away. And with it, the cold sensation of the steel against his skin was gone as well.

Chikai aimed the gun at Kamome's still body and pulled the trigger.

Bang! Bang!

The ear-splitting sound broke his paralysis. He glanced up at his brother, who stared at Kamome's corpse without an ounce of emotion on his face.

"In this world, it's only the bad people who survive." Chikai knelt down so he was at eye level with Toi. He gave his little brother a smile for the first time. "I'm the one who killed him. With this gun."

"Huh?" he gasped in shock.

"The two of us are going to survive this world, no matter what it takes. You understand, right?" Chikai squeezed his arms tight around Toi.

It was the first time that had ever happened.

Toi clung to Chikai, whose back felt so broad that no matter how much Toi stretched, he couldn't fully wrap his arms around his older brother. He felt embarrassed by how young he was—helpless, weak, unable to do anything but stand around and be protected.

"Yeah...yeah!" Toi said finally as hot tears bubbled up, wetting his frozen cheeks.

Never again would the two of them be separated. They swore as much that day.

"No!"

His sorrowful cry echoed in their shared ocean of emotions.

After the Desire Field faded, Toi noticed he had a new message on his phone.

Chikai: The situation's changed, doesn't look like I'll be able to come back. I'll contact you again later.

A few short, curt sentences. His brother had dished out similar bad news countless times before. Today's, however, was particularly disheartening.

"Unfortunately, today's Wishing Plate is silver once again, ribbit."

"Tch..." Toi snatched the proffered dish up, but when he tried to leave, Enta stopped him.

"H-hey, hold on a second! I saw what happened. Toi, you... that guy..."

"Yeah. I killed someone," Toi finished for him.

"How can you...how can you be so cool about it?"

There was no point in trying to argue about it, at least not in Toi's mind. He had no interest in associating with these two anyway, so it was best for them to hurry up and distance themselves. "If I hadn't shot him, then he might have killed me. Or he would have killed my brother."

"Still—" Enta started to protest.

"You want to argue *so bad* over whether it was justified or not, go ahead. But concepts like good and evil don't mean squat to the powerful. That's why I decided that I need to get strong, so I can survive and stay with my brother. I can take whatever judgment you want to dish out, I don't care."

"But..."

"But I won't allow anyone to put my brother's sacrifice to waste. If you spill my secret..."

In the blink of an eye, Toi whipped his ruler out, grazing the tip of Enta's nose. The other boy squeaked in surprise.

"I'll run you through."

Toi left the collapsed Enta behind and started to leave the plaza.

"Kuji!"

He didn't need any more trouble. But no sooner had he thought that than Kazuki came running after him.

"Here, my Wishing Plate. You can have it."

"Kazuki?!" Enta exclaimed, crawling after them on his hands and knees.

Toi glanced at the silver Wishing Plate and then at Kazuki's face. "What's this about?"

"I think you deserve this more than I do."

Enta couldn't hold his tongue after hearing that. "What are you talking about?! You've been doing all of this for Haruka, right?! Why are you handing your plate over to someone like Kuji, of all people?! Isn't Haruka important to you?"

"I..." Kazuki balled up his fists, squeezing out the words. "I hate Haruka."

PLATE 5

Sachet

SCENE 1

KAZUKI WAS FIVE at the time.

It was a bright, sunny afternoon at the beginning of spring when the Yasakas brought home the fourth member of their family. Their living room overlooked the Sumida River, lined with sakura trees that blossomed beautifully in the spring. They decided to name the little boy Haruka, after the Japanese word for the season that was upon them.

"...Haruka," Kazuki said softly, testing the name.

Kazuki could see his reflection in the baby's misty eyes. Haruka's hand, smaller than an autumn leaf, stretched slowly toward him. When he reached his out in return, the baby clasped his finger tightly. Kazuki was surprised at the strength of his little brother's grip, and he felt a sense of duty, one he couldn't describe in words, swell in his chest.

Kazuki's father, who watched from beside him, wrapped his arm around Kazuki's shoulder and said, "You're an older brother now."

That's when it hit him.

That's right, I am *an older brother now!*

Kazuki felt joy then, at meeting someone that he needed to protect. He gently leaned his face in toward Haruka's. The baby smelled of sweet milk and sunshine.

Ever since that day, the two of them were always together.

Haruka's first word was "Kaa-cha," a nickname that sounded similar to the Japanese word for mother (Kaa-chan). This led to a disagreement in which their mother insisted Haruka was calling her name, while Kazuki swore it was his name. The boys' father, looking rather dejected, had to play peacemaker.

One day, their happiness was abruptly cut short.

Kazuki was ten years old when his grandfather on his dad's side became terminally ill. As all of his relatives gathered at his grandfather's bedside, the old man suddenly pointed his finger at Kazuki and said, "Your real mother was a disaster."

For a moment, Kazuki had no idea what he meant. He could tell, however, from the chilly air around him, that the woman beside him was *not* who his grandfather meant. As he stood there, dazed, he understood that he didn't belong. The only saving grace of the situation had been that Haruka slept through it all and hadn't heard a peep.

He had a *real* mother out there; one he had been ripped away from. His parents were tight-lipped about the details, but they eventually told him that he was actually the child of his father's older brother.

"Still, that doesn't change the fact that the four of us are a family," his father gently assured him. Kazuki tried to believe him.

But we're not really family. I'm the only one who isn't connected to them. Such thoughts came daily, unbidden, flitting through his head again and again.

Suddenly, everything that they shared up until now—matching striped outfits for the whole family, the four of them gathered at the table for a piping hot breakfast—he could no longer enjoy sincerely. Just seeing Haruka's face, as the younger boy innocently idolized him, felt painful for Kazuki. He no longer knew the scent of happiness.

Sarazanmai

PLATE 5

Sachet

SCENE 2

THE KAMINARI 5656 MEETING HALL, located in Asakusa and owned by the Tokiwadou Kaminari Okoshi Head Office, was a performance hall with a long history. It had a flashy exterior and a traditional arched roof, like something straight out of a Japanese fairy tale. This was where the local idol Azuma Sara's meet-and-greet event was to be held that day.

"It's here! That's Sara's car!" Kazuki said as he watched the van slip into the parking lot. He hefted the box holding his Sara disguise in his hands.

"Hey, are we seriously doing this?" asked Toi, who'd let himself get wrapped up in this despite his reservations.

"Of course we are! I'm going to see this mission through to the end!" They even labeled the mission "Operation Kidnap Azuma Sara."

"Why are you like this?"

At Toi's question, Kazuki looked confused. "Huh? Oh, you mean why I'm not dressed up yet? I'm going to change after—"

"No, not that! I mean, you know about me now... Why haven't you said anything?"

137

Seeing how awkward Toi was acting, Kazuki dropped the tone of his voice a bit and said, "I was scared at first, but I was also jealous of you. Incredibly jealous."

"What the...? I don't get you at all."

"Yeah, sorry. I know it's probably all just me being selfish."

The expression on Toi's face made it clear that he didn't understand.

"All right, let's go," said Kazuki, trying to switch gears. "First we have to deal with the manager."

"Okay, Sara, I'll come get you ten minutes before it's time to go on stage," the manager said as he ducked out of her dressing room.

"Roger that, dish ☆," she called back, sounding just as dreamy as she did on TV.

Toi took one glance at the door, labeled "Azuma Sara's Dressing Room," and promptly followed after the manager.

"Hm-hmm, hum. ♪" The manager was in a cheerful mood as he relieved himself inside the old-style bathroom. "Sara's finally gotten popular enough to hold her own personal event at the 5656 Meeting Hall. If we keep this up, we might actually make it to the Budokan arena one day!" He continued muttering about his dreams of grandeur, trying to slide up his zipper when—

Creaaaaak.

He could hear the door to one of the stalls behind him crack open.

"Hm?"

In the mirror in front of him, the manager watched as a man in a kappa mask whipped out a cucumber.

138

"Gyaaaah?! Guh?! Urgh?!"

A sign hung on the door to the men's bathroom that read *Closed for Cleaning*. The noises echoing from behind the door certainly seemed disturbing for a simple cleaning, but silence settled back over the area soon enough.

"Phew…" Toi pulled the mask to the side of his face and heaved a sigh. In the stall in front of him sat the manager, bound and pantsless, looking utterly depraved.

"What the heck am I doing…?" Toi's complaint slipped out the bathroom window along with the man's pants, disappearing in the wind.

Sara lifted her head at hearing a knock on the door. The smartphone in her hand displayed the thumbnails for a series of cucumber photos: the phrase "cucumbers around the world" had been typed into the search engine above.

"Pardon the intrusion." The person who entered the room wore a kappa mask on his face.

If Sara were a normal idol, she would have immediately called for help after an intruder slipped into her room. As fate would have it, however, the man in the kappa mask held the very cucumber in his hand that he used in his crime moments ago.

"It's a cucumber, dish! ☆" she said happily.

"We'd like you to do a PR photoshoot before you go on stage for the meet-and-greet." He gestured with the cucumber, and Sara's eyes followed it greedily. She was too focused on it to question his request.

"Okay, dish. ☆"

Toi sighed behind his kappa mask, a little surprised at how easily he managed to lure her out of the room with him.

"What the heck am I doing...?" he muttered, not for the first time today, though no one paid attention to his complaint.

One person watched Toi's careful execution of the plan—Sara-Kazuki. "Kuji, you did it!" He stepped out of the shadows and slipped into Sara's waiting room, safe and unnoticed.

"Okay, everything's in place," Kazuki told himself. As he sat at the extravagant vanity, his smartphone chirped at him, alerting him of a new message.

Harukappa: I just arrived at the meeting hall! I'll finally be able to meet you! A selfie of Haruka in front of the venue was attached to the text.

Sara: Thanks for coming! I am excited to meet you too, dish! ☆

Harukappa: Remember how we talked about a secret code yesterday? I thought of a good one!

Sara: Okay, tell me!

Sara-Kazuki's expression remained dark the whole time, at odds with the cheerful replies he was sending. The words Toi said to him before replayed through his mind: *You and I aren't so different. We're the kind of people who'll do anything to get what we want.* Toi couldn't have been more right.

Kazuki dressed up as Haruka's favorite female idol, created a fake account to connect with his little brother, and even went so far as kidnapping Sara today so he could fulfill his promise. *All for Haruka.*

Even I know this is insane, he thought.

Harukappa: I'll say, "From beginning to end." And you'll say, "We're all connected in a great big circle"

Kazuki's fingers trembled as he typed his reply.

Sara: That's a beautiful secret code, dish! ☆

Harukappa: It's a sign that we're connected!

After he read Haruka's reply, Sara-Kazuki hugged the phone tightly against his chest. Then he lifted his face, all traces of doubt gone now.

Real or not, Haruka and I are still connected.

The fifth and sixth floors of the 5656 Meeting Hall were one giant, open area, an enormous room with a stage that was called Tokiwa Hall. There was a line of fans at the entrance, waiting for the venue to open.

Enta stood beside Haruka and his parents. He glanced down at the boy, who was gazing intently at the screen of his smartphone. "Haruka, what are you watching?"

"It's today's lucky selfie horoscope!" On the tiny screen of the device, Sara was announcing the item of the day.

"You must really like her to be watching this when you're about to meet her in person in a few minutes."

"Yeah! I love her!"

Behind the screen, Sara's dreamy voice intoned, *"Now then, what will today's lucky selfie item be? It's a sachet, dish!* ☆*"*

Haruka looked back at his mother and asked, "Hey, what's a 'sachet'?"

"It's a fragrance bag, filled with scented potpourri."

"A fragrance bag..." Haruka echoed. A tremor seemed to run through his body, though it went unnoticed by both his parents and Enta.

Enta cut in and said, "S-so Kazuki didn't come with you guys today?"

"No," said Haruka's mother. "Kazu-kun left early this morning."

"O-oh, okay..." Enta pasted a strained smile onto his face to mask his inner panic. *What the heck are you doing, Kazuki?! If Haruka finds out the truth, it's all over!*

"Okay then," came Sara's voice from Haruka's phone. "Have a wonderful day, and may lots of luck be dished your way! ☆"

PLATE 5

Sachet

SCENE 3

AN IMPOSING HUSH settled over the large conference room at the Asakusa Police Station, where a meeting was presently underway. A paper on the outside of the door read: *Asakusa Suspicious Death Investigation HQ.*

The chief's voice echoed inside the dimly lit room. "We have identified the body we found early this morning: unemployed thirty-five-year-old Nioino Fukuro." His profile revealed that his name was written with the kanji for "fragrance bag." "Six months ago, we arrested him as a suspect in connection with the Asakusa Protected Species Fragrance Bag Incident. He was released after we failed to bring charges against him. We'll be investigating his death as a homicide."

There was an audible *ka-chik* as the projector flipped through photos of multiple Japanese giant salamanders—listed as a protected species—that had been unlawfully abducted and imprisoned in cages. These same salamanders were, of all things, being fed curry so their sweat could be extracted.

The prevailing mood in the room was pretty much, *Come on,*

there's no way a potpourri with their sweat could make for a good fragrance bag. There was a fiery energy in the room.

In the midst of all of this, two people abruptly stood up—Reo and Mabu.

"We're the ones who sniffed him out!" said Reo.

"It was yesterday's sachet!" said Mabu.

Yesterday evening, to be precise. The incident took place at the police box where the two worked.

"This is a stinkin' false arrest!"

"For those souls without beginnings or ends, those unable to connect..." Mabu held up a photo of Nioino at the scene of the crime, feeding extremely spicy curry to a giant salamander sitting in a bucket.

"Now, let us open a door..." Reo aimed the barrel of his gun at the man. "Is it desire?"

"Or love?"

A large taiko drum appeared above Nioino's head.

"Desire Extraction!"

Nioino was absorbed into the drum and disappeared completely.

"This is where we'll do the shoot. Please go on in."

The man in the kappa mask brought Sara to a nearby building, called Asakusa Kannon Hot Spring. The vines covering the building's exterior gave it a solemn atmosphere, but it had actually closed its doors for good. Behind the creaking entry lay a dark, vast skeleton of a once-booming business.

"Ooh... This feels like something straight out of a horror move, dish. ☆" Sara, who was not like other idols, stepped inside without an ounce of suspicion. And as soon as she did, the door slammed closed behind her.

The culprit, of course, was the man in the kappa mask—Toi. He wrapped a heavy chain around the outside of the door, then inserted a key into the giant lock on the front, effectively sealing the girl inside.

"I'll let you out as soon as the handshake event is over. If you wanna hold this against anyone, hold it against *him*, not me." Feeling satisfied that his work was done, he glanced behind him to discover—

"A com*plate*ly successful escape! ☆" There stood Azuma Sara, in her trademark pose.

"What?! Why—how did you get out?!" He glanced back, but of course the padlock and chain were perfectly intact.

Toi chased after her, and soon found himself trapped in a cat-and-mouse game with him trapping her and her slithering free. He tried sealing her in a telephone box, a large coin locker, and finally even a magic box with swords sticking out of it. But no matter where he locked her up, she always snuck out to declare, "A com*plate*ly successful escape! ☆"

Toi, who had some experience in criminal activity, lost all of his confidence at this utter defeat. "Just what the heck is she?!"

"And now we'll commence the meet-and-greet with Asakusa's very own idol, Azuma Sara-san!" The announcement echoed throughout the event hall, finally heralding Sara's long-awaited appearance.

It was Enta's first time ever seeing her in person, and his nerves made him lose sight of his original objective—to prevent Kazuki's secret from being revealed.

At least until he saw Sara-Kazuki appear on stage.

"Good morning! ☆ It's me, Azuma Sara, dish! ☆"

Whoa, whoa, whoa, are you seriously doing this?! Enta was completely flabbergasted, unable to believe that Kazuki would resort to something like this. But he quickly remembered his mission. *No! Haruka's going to realize the truth!*

Just as he outstretched his hands to try to cover the younger boy's eyes, Haruka exclaimed, "It's Sara-chan! She's sooo cute!"

"Huh?"

It wasn't just Haruka either; cheers erupted from all over the audience.

Th-they're all buying it?!

Sara-Kazuki responded to their encouraging shouts with a smile. "I am so glad you all came here today, dish. ☆ I was really looking forward to meeting you as we—huh?!" His eyes met Enta's. He was clearly shaken by the sight of his friend in the crowd.

Enta used the hand signs they created back when they played soccer together to send a message. *Haruka doesn't know. Keep going.* Who would have guessed they'd ever use those signs under these circumstances?

The meet-and-greet proceeded smoothly, until at last it was Enta's turn. Haruka was waiting behind him.

"I'm cheering for you. In more ways than one..." Enta said sincerely, offering his genuine support.

"I-I appreciate that, dish... ☆" Sara-Kazuki smiled awkwardly and shook his hand.

Their father pushed Haruka forward in his wheelchair, until he was sitting right before Sara-Kazuki.

"Sara-chan!" Haruka tightly gripped both of Sara-Kazuki's hands, their warmth the same as they had been that day.

Sarazanmai

PLATE 5

Sachet

SCENE 4

UNABLE TO SHAKE OFF the unease he felt since his grandfather's death, Kazuki began playing soccer. He had no particular love for the sport; he just wanted an excuse not to be at home. It worked better than expected, since he became so immersed in the game that he could forget about everything else.

Regardless of why he started playing, Kazuki still developed a genuine love for the sport. Soon, his and Haruka's shared bedroom was covered in soccer merch and posters of overseas players.

Playing gave him the strength to stop wearing matching outfits with his family. The season was changing, and with it, the clothes everyone wore. Kazuki wondered what his parents must have thought when he threw the striped outfit into the trash.

He spent the rest of the day playing soccer by himself at the park in front of their condo complex.

"Kazu-chan!"

He somehow knew it would be Haruka that came to get him.

Kazuki stopped practicing and climbed up the whale-shaped jungle gym. His brother scaled up after him, and the two sat side-by-side at the top.

"I saw you from the veranda, and thought I'd come say hi!"

In front of them, the sakura trees were in full blossom, with Skytree looming up in the distance. Just beyond the promenade sat the Sumida River, its water quiet that spring night.

Kazuki felt a prick of guilt, and unable to hold his silence any longer, finally asked, "Were Mom and Dad mad?"

"Nope. They're not mad, but they *are* worried. Worried that you've never really liked wearing matching outfits with us. Do you really...hate it that much?"

Yes, completely.

"No, it's not that. But I'll be in middle school soon. It's time I grow out of that kinda stuff." Kazuki's excuse was sloppy, thrown out to brush his brother off, but Haruka seemed to buy it.

"Ohh, okay. You're already an adult, huh...?"

If only that were true, then he could live on his own. Right now, though, Kazuki was just a helpless child.

"But you know..." Haruka took Kazuki's hand in his. "Even if we wear different clothes, even if you grow up and we're not together anymore, we're all still connected by a great big circle, from beginning to end."

Even now, Kazuki still remembered the warmth he felt from Haruka's hand.

"From beginning to end!"

Haruka's words brought him jolting back to reality. This was Sara's meet-and-greet, and right now *he* was Sara. He had to respond with Haruka's secret code.

"We're all connected...in a great big circle." It was a struggle to squeeze the words out, and he wondered if his voice wavered.

"Ehehe! Thank you!" When Haruka smiled blithely at him, Kazuki swore he heard a creaking sound, as if his heart was bending, warping inside his chest. And then—

"That Sara's a fake!" Sara's manager reappeared, bursting through a door on the side of the stage.

Throughout the event center, noise erupted from the crowd. It was little wonder why; the manager wasn't wearing any pants.

"A fake?" Haruka murmured.

"Where's the *real* Sara?!" The manager shrieked.

Enta flung himself at the man, trying to hold him back. "Gah! This guy's a pervert—a flasher! Watch out, Sara-chan!"

"Urgh! What are you doing?! Get off me, four-eyes!"

"Oh, stuff it! You wear glasses too!" Enta protested.

As the two quarreled, Haruka argued, "*This* is the real Sara-chan! She has to be, she said the secret code!" Kazuki had never seen his little brother speak so fiercely to someone before. Neither had his parents, he was sure.

Everyone was taken aback at the sudden disruption.

"Oh dear. What's going on, dish?" A dreamy voice echoed from the back. There, at the exit farthest from the stage, stood Azuma Sara. Behind her, hunched over and breathless, was Toi.

"Huh? There's...two of them?" Haruka stared at her in disbelief.

"Sara-chan! You're all right!" exclaimed the manager.

"I went out for a cup of fresh air, dish." Sara seemed completely unaware of the fact that someone had attempted to abduct and confine her.

As she merrily made her way to the stage, Haruka shouted at her, "From beginning to end!"

"Hm?"

"It's my secret code with Sara-chan!"

Of course, there was no way for the real Sara to know what he meant.

"And...you are?" she asked.

The boy's expression changed in an instant. "I knew it, you're the fake! Right, Sara-cha—" Haruka whipped his head around to face who he thought was the real Sara, but the manager ripped her wig off, revealing his older brother, Kazuki. "Kazu-chan...?"

Though he stood on a stage bathed in lights, Kazuki's vision went completely dark.

Chaos erupted in the event center, but on the stage itself, an eerie quiet settled.

"Kazu-chan... Ah!" Just as Haruka called his brother's name, a small bag from inside his pocket floated up through the air before soaring off into the distance. "That's my...!" The boy reached his hand out for it, but it had already floated out of reach.

Enta, who had been with the manager, watched it go. "Don't tell me there's another Kappa Zombie?!"

Kazuki took advantage of Haruka's distraction to snatch up his wig and retreat from the stage. Only his headdress, which he hadn't had time to retrieve, was left behind.

Haruka called after him. "Wait! Kazu-chan...!"

But Kazuki ran as fast as he could, as though he could outrun the echo of his brother's voice.

Sarazanmai

PLATE 5

––∞∞∞∞∞∞∞––

Sachet

SCENE 5

ENTA ARRIVED at their usual spot—the Kappa Plaza. He found Kazuki, as expected, still dressed in his Sara outfit, his back facing Enta.

"Kazuki," Enta started to say.

Kazuki let the wig slip from his hands, and it hit the ground with a soft *fwump*. "It's over. Everything I've done, all of it..."

There was nothing Enta could say. He knew exactly how Kazuki felt, to a painful degree.

"You knew he'd find out eventually. That day just happened to be today," said Toi, breaking the silence.

"Kuji...!"

"Everything people try to hide gets found out eventually. That's all there is to it. It happens to all of us."

Toi said it perfectly. Enta had struggled desperately to keep his feelings for Kazuki a secret. When it leaked out that Enta kissed Kazuki when he was sleeping, Enta resigned himself to believing that this was the end.

"This was foolish from the start," continued Toi. "Did you really think you could keep it a secret forever?"

"Enough already!" Enta snapped at him, tired of hearing it.

Toi, however, ignored him and continued pressing Kazuki. "Why are you pretending to be the victim? *You're* the one who did this, the one who hurt your little brother. You're the perpetrator!"

Kazuki's shoulders jolted, and in the same instant, Enta seized Toi. "He doesn't need to hear that from a murderer like you!"

But the moment Enta said that, he realized something. Toi's words hadn't just been meant for Kazuki—he was speaking to himself as well. Still, Enta couldn't back down now.

Nor could Toi.

"Then you tell him! If you're really some 'Golden Duo,' then knock some sense into him already!"

"I..." They were both glaring at one another, each with a fistful of the other person's shirt in their hand, when Kazuki's voice broke through and caught their attention. "I'm the one who hurt Haruka. Even though I swore the first time would be the last, I'm the one who hurt him again."

"Kazuki..."

"Again?" Toi whispered quietly, only for his voice to be blown away as Keppi wailed.

"Desiiiire...Extractioooon!"

In the next instant, all three of them had been turned into kappa.

"That was really rude, doing that out of nowhere, Keppi!" Kappa-Enta complained.

"Kappa Zombies come out when it gets dark. Thus, I changed you into kappa. Is there a problem with that, ribbit?"

Toi replied, "Yeah, this whole thing is a problem, actually."

Noticing Kazuki's silence, Kappa-Enta tried to change the subject out of consideration. "So, the thing that Haruka swiped from him... Uh, what are those things called again?"

"This Kappa Zombie's desire is for fragrance bags, ribbit."

"Yeah, that's what they're called! If it's something really important to Haruka, we definitely have to get it back! Right, Kazuki?"

After a moment of silence, Kappa-Kazuki just gave a small nod.

"Kappature it!" Keppi cried as the three of them flew toward the creature.

"This sachet smells good~!" The Kappa Zombie mercilessly showered them in a pleasant fragrance.

"Ooh, it *does* smell good..." murmured the three. It rendered them lightheaded, unable to draw out their usual power.

"Memories of smell remain until death! I want to drown myself in her scent!"

Fortunately, they were still able to successfully stop the creature's onslaught. Then, with Kazuki at the forefront of their attack, they plunged toward the Zombie's butthole.

"You can't rely on something you can't see!" shouted Kappa-Kazuki.

"Gyaaaah!"

"We kappatured it!" they yelled in unison.

As Kazuki held the creature's shirikodama, he was shown a vision of the man's desire, of his girlfriend peeling off her boots and smearing her feet over his nose.

"Aah... Spicy..." said the man.

"So that's it," Kappa-Kazuki realized, "you were searching for the smell of someone you cared about."

"My secret's been sniffed ooooooout!"

Nioino's Kappa Zombie body began to fracture.

"Saraaa!"

"Saraaa!"

"Saraaa!"

And then all together, "Sarazanmai!"

"Leaking."

The first scene, as Kazuki's secret began to flow through their minds, was of him and Haruka by the whale-shaped jungle gym.

"Even if we wear different clothes, even if you grow up and we're not together anymore, we're all still connected by a great big circle, from beginning to end."

"Haruka..."

"Ehehe! Kazu-chan, let's go home together, okay?"

Haruka's words brought him back to his real family. After that, Kazuki recovered the striped clothes he'd thrown out. His parents watched with a look of relief on their faces. Their daily lives returned to normal, as if nothing had ever happened. Kazuki immersed himself in soccer, improving his skills until he and Enta were considered the Golden Duo.

Days and months passed. The color of the soccer posters on

his wall faded quite a bit. One day, during spring break just before his second year in junior high, he met a woman as he was headed home after soccer practice.

"Kazuki…!"

When she softly wrapped her arms around him in a hug, he caught the scent of sakura—a smell that was like a key unlocking his distant memories. He had no memory of meeting her before, yet her smell was so familiar to him.

"…Mom?"

His birth mother was carrying a fragrance bag on her that smelled like sakura.

"Why are you…?"

As Kazuki watched this replay of his memories, he realized that *this* was the bag his brother had been carrying in his pocket. The one that flew away when the Kappa Zombie showed up.

"Why was Haruka carrying my mom's fragrance bag? Unless…!"

Normally the shirikodama would pass from each one of them, but instead it went flying out from Kappa-Kazuki's rear, only to be reabsorbed by the Kappa Zombie.

"I got it baaaack!"

This was the first time they ever failed a mission.

Tink, tink, tink…

Water was boiling in an earthenware kettle, causing the lid to clink noisily.

"You didn't defeat the Kappa Zombie, so there will be no Wishing Plate today, ribbit. You idiots have made me so angry I'm boiling tea on my belly button! Ribbit!" Keppi wasn't speaking figuratively either: there was quite literally a kettle of tea boiling on his belly button. "And, of course, you cannot return to your human forms, ribbit."

"What?!"

"Tch..."

Enta and Toi, now stuck in their kappa forms, were none too pleased by this development.

"I'm fine staying like this," Kappa-Kazuki muttered.

"Wh-what are you saying?" Enta demanded.

"Haruka must have known... He must've known we weren't real brothers!"

Kazuki explained what had happened after the flash of memory he leaked to Enta and Toi.

PLATE 5

Sachet

SCENE 6

"**Y**OU'RE IN THE SOCCER CLUB? And you're a forward? That's incredible!" His mother appeared out of nowhere, but she was beautiful, kind, and full of smiles. Kazuki struggled to hide his confusion at first, but as they spoke, his reservations gradually subsided.

When Kazuki was young, he worried that his real mother was actually a horrible person after all. As he grew older, he became more certain that she was as awful as he feared, but his fretting just motivated him to cherish his current family even more.

In truth, shortly after Kazuki was born, her husband—his birth father—had died in an accident. Kazuki's anxious grandfather pressured her to give her baby up. Knowing the full story about how he'd been adopted, Kazuki couldn't find it in him to blame anyone.

"Honestly, I was so immature back then," his mother said. "I lost the person I loved, and it was like my world turned pitch black. All I wanted to do was run from the pain of reality. But after we were separated, I thought about you all the time."

His mother spared no detail in explaining why, exactly, she had come to see him. She even disclosed the specifics of her current situation. "Actually, I have a family now that's just as important to me as you are. I know it's very selfish of me, but I still desperately wanted to see you," she said, embracing him.

He could no longer catch the scent of sakura anymore. Instead, he remembered the scent of sweet milk and sunshine. "I have family that's important to me too. And a really adorable younger brother," he said.

"Kazuki..."

He wondered what she thought. Kazuki couldn't tell for certain, but the two of them smiled at each other. He said, "Let's keep our reunion a secret. And tomorrow when you leave from the station, I'll go to see you off."

"All right."

He felt more at peace than he ever had before, honestly happy from the bottom of his heart. Kazuki was part of a real and beautiful family, even if he hadn't been born into it.

The next morning, he carefully snuck out of his house before anyone could see he was awake. His birth mother was taking a long train ride from the Tokyo Skytree station back to her family. After mulling it over the whole night, Kazuki decided that his current family was, truly, the most important thing in his life. That was why he wanted to keep his meeting with his birth mother a secret, so as not to worry them. Yet despite all his caution—

"Kazu-chan!"

He was waiting at a busy intersection on the east side of the Azuma Bridge when his brother came racing down the bridge toward him.

"Haruka, why are you here?"

The younger boy finally caught up, completely out of breath. "Where are you going? I'm going too!"

"You can't." He was going to see his birth mother off. There was no way he could bring Haruka along.

"Why not? Is it because I've been bad?!" Haruka sometimes worried that he was being punished for something he didn't know he'd done.

"I never said that." *And I have to hurry,* Kazuki thought. The time for his mother's train departure was fast approaching.

"I'm sorry! I'm sorry! I'll be good from now, so...don't leave, Kazu-chan!"

"Enough!" Kazuki impulsively batted his little brother's hand away.

"Ah...!"

They both inhaled sharply at the same time, as Kazuki realized what he'd done and Haruka processed the rejection. But Kazuki was out of time. He had to leave his brother behind or he'd never see his mother again.

At some point, the light turned green. Kazuki hardened his heart and started to make his way across the crosswalk. The pedestrian sign began to flash, signaling that the light would change again soon.

"Wait...wait! Kazu-chan...!"

He had no real memory of what happened after that. Just vague things, like the dark shade of the pedestrian light, the

sunlight pouring over the street from the west, the growing pud-
dle of painfully vibrant red. Red. *RED*. It all played out in slow
motion, as if he were in an underwater world. And ever since that
moment, Kazuki couldn't breathe properly.

The Kappa Plaza was dead silent, almost like the bottom of
the ocean.

Kappa-Kazuki's voice was so uncertain, so broken, that the
words came out like bubbles, floating up and disappearing. "I
felt so much regret... It's just like Kuji said, *I* am the perpetrator.
Haruka will never walk again."

"But...but..." Unsurprisingly, Kappa-Enta was the first who
steeled his will to speak up. "I don't know how to say this, but...
you're not responsible for what happened, Kazuki."

"Everyone told me the same thing. My dad, my mom...even
Haruka!"

Enta went quiet after Kazuki said that.

"No one blamed me! Even though I'm the one who ruined
everything!"

Kappa-Toi just watched quietly.

"That's why I decided to punish myself. I decided we'd stay a
fake family forever. But they all keep trying to treat me like I'm
really part of their family."

Tears welled up in Enta's eyes. It was as if Kazuki were telling
them that he'd never let anyone else in his heart ever again.

"Every time I see Haruka's wheelchair, I can't breathe. I quit
playing soccer, but it's just not enough. So I stole Nyantaro.

I even became Sara so I could be connected to Haruka...!" As he spoke the last of his confession to them, Kazuki's eyes filled with tears. Everything he said was the truth, one he kept hidden from everyone until now. One he'd turned his back on for so long—his true, bleak, dreary self.

"Saying it was all for Haruka is a lie. I...I deceived Haruka to protect myself. I..."

He wanted to be connected, even if he had no right to be.

Sarazanmai

PLATE 6

Haruka

SCENE 1

IT HAPPENED YESTERDAY. Yesterday evening, to be precise.

"Glad our zombie this time is a tough one." Reo and Mabu zoomed through the air on an underground elevator. Reo seemed to be in a good mood as he fiddled with the photograph in his hand. Nioino was still visible in the picture.

"Indeed. I can finally leave the station," said Mabu.

Reo's expression soured. "What? Maintenance? *Again?*"

"Yes. It's a matter of life or death for me." Mabu's tone remained entirely even, either unaware of or ignoring the sudden shift in Reo's mood.

"Pfft, yeah, I wonder about that! You sure you're not just hooked on it because it feels good?" As Reo flung words dripping with sarcasm at his partner, the elevator arrived at its destination—the inside of their police box.

Mabu immediately headed for the door. "Absurd. What benefit would there be in prioritizing my personal feelings?" He turned and disappeared into the darkness of the night.

Once his partner was gone, Reo slammed his fist against the wall. "As if you could ever understand even an ounce of what I'm feeling!"

167

Sarazanmai

PLATE 6

Haruka

SCENE 2

"**G**OOD MORNING! ☆ Every day is happy! And with your lucky selfie, you'll have even more happiness on your plate! It's me, Azuma Sara, dish! ☆"

The living room filled with the sound of Sara's voice as her Asakusa Sara TV segment began, but their morning routine lacked its normal liveliness. Haruka never ventured over to the breakfast table, but silently watched the television, instead.

His father looked on and asked, "Have you heard anything from Kazuki?"

Haruka's mother shook her head, holding a coffee cup in either hand. "Not since I got a message last night that he's staying over at Enta-kun's house."

"All right." There was a brief pause before he continued, "Now that I think about it, she does kind of resemble him." His eyes were turned toward the screen, where Sara was dancing.

"Yes. Maybe that's why Haruka became such a big fan."

"Now then, what will today's lucky selfie item be?" droned Sara's voice in the background.

Neither of Haruka's parents could see the expression on the boy's face.

"Oh dear, what's this?" Sara sounded confused. *"It looks like today's item is a sachet too, dish."*

A headdress decorated with ribbons rested in Haruka's lap. Yesterday, after Kazuki took off running, the real Sara had picked it up and handed it to him. There she'd been, the idol he adored so much, right before his eyes...and he'd barely noticed. He just murmured, "Thanks." Sara offered him a gentle nod in return.

"Okay then, have a wonderful day, and may you have lots of luck dished your way! ☆*"* said the Sara on the television.

"Kazu-chan..."

Krunch, krunch, krunch, krunch, krunch, krunch...

Toi and Enta were standing in the Kappa Plaza, still in their kappa forms, and utterly speechless at what they were witnessing. Before their eyes, Kappa-Kazuki was binge eating a literal mountain of cucumbers.

"Cucumbers are delicious! They taste even better now than when I was human!" Kazuki continued to be in unusually high spirits.

Toi gave him a look of pity. "He's lost it."

"It's a Kappa High, ribbit," Keppi explained. "A euphoria that occurs when someone remains a kappa for a prolonged period of time, ribbit." He was equally at a loss for what to do.

In the meantime, Kazuki continued to munch away at his cucumbers. "Being a kappa rules!"

Du-dun, dun, dun, dun...
"To the eeeast, Kazuki no Umi. To the weeest, Enta Yama!" Keppi's high voice rang through the air, mimicking the referee's style of speech from sumo matches. In the center of the plaza appeared a wrestling ring, joined by the delightful, rhythmic sound of taiko drums. "Eyes on your opponent!"

Kappa-Enta lifted his knee up high and stomped down, his hair tied up in a topknot. "Uh, does sumo have *anything* to do with our current predicament?"

In front of him, Kappa-Kazuki braced himself for the match, sporting a similar hairstyle. "It has absolutely everything to do with it!"

"Still safe, still safe, still safe~!"

The two grappled with each other, kappa-lately evenly matched and struggling for the upper hand. Sweat slowly beaded on their skin. The droplets made quiet *plip, plip* sounds as they sprinkled across the ground.

Ah, ahh! Kazuki's skin is rubbing up against mine... Enta's expression suggested he was in the throes of ecstasy. In contrast, Kazuki looked entirely serious about their match.

"Show me what you're made of, Enta."

"K-Kazuki...!"

Plip, plip, plip. Their skin grew even more slippery.

"I-I can't...take it any—"

"That's pathetic, Enta! We're the Golden Duo, aren't we?!" Kappa-Kazuki pressed his knee hard against Enta's crotch.

"Aaaaaaah~!"

Kappa-Enta went soaring through the air, landing outside the ring. When he hit the ground, Enta realized that this must have been another one of his delusions.

"Enta!"

But for some reason, it didn't just end there as it usually did.

"Are you okay? You aren't hurt?" Kazuki looked handsome and suave as he reached out for Enta.

"Huh? Wait, is this a delusion too...?"

Keppi offered him a pack of gum with only a single stick of gum left. *Pa-chink!* When Enta grabbed the gum, a trap attached to it came swinging down, pinching his finger.

"Ouch! It's not a delusion!"

Keppi, still dressed in his sumo referee outfit, gave a quiet nod.

"Being a kappa rules!" Kappa-Enta and Kappa-Kazuki shouted in unison.

"Ribbit!"

Behind the three, who had thrown their arms around one another's shoulders, Kappa-Toi was busily sweeping up the sumo ring.

"Time for our next piece of news, dish! ☆ The police reported that an investigation is ongoing regarding the fragrance bag theft that began yesterday. They currently believe the crime is a large-scale operation." The nightly news was playing on a large monitor hanging on the front of the Asakusa Culture and Tourism Information Center.

Kappa-Toi looked up to watch and mumbled to himself, "Have any of the incidents before made it on the news the day after?"

"Come to think of it, no, they haven't—ack, no!" Kappa-Enta replied on impulse, but then immediately forced his mouth shut. The two had been at each other's throats since this whole thing began. Their current ceasefire had only happened because they'd been turned into kappa and kept too busy to resume fighting. Granted, judging by Toi's demeanor, he wasn't the least bit concerned about the unresolved conflict.

Enta, however, wasn't ready to bury the hatchet. "Hmph!"

Kappa-Toi just watched in exasperation as the other boy made an obvious show of giving him the cold shoulder.

"Oh hey! No one can see us in our kappa forms, which means we've basically got a free pass to Hanayashiki, right?"

It was just like Enta to suggest such a thing. The group made their way to the small playground with a multipurpose bathroom.

"Oh, there's a soccer ball here!" Kappa-Enta exclaimed. He ran over to it and began playing.

"This place is..." Kappa-Toi's voice trailed off as he realized where they were.

Kazuki smiled and replied, "Yeah, this is where I always came to change into my Sara costume. I mean, so hilariously stupid, right? Cross-dressing as an idol!"

"You put a lot of effort into it though," said Toi.

"Enough, it's over. Anyway, let's just have fun! Being a kappa rules!"

Toi watched him go with a sigh. It was obvious that Kazuki was just putting on a brave face.

Kappa-Enta continued dribbling the soccer ball, all the while piecing together a magnificent plan in his mind. Although it was true Kazuki was putting on a façade, he was still full of energy today. *Which means that maybe if I play it smooth, I can pass him the ball...*

"Heey! Enta!"

He glanced back to see Kappa-Kazuki racing toward him. "Pass it to me!"

"Really? I thought you said soccer didn't have anything to do with you anymore."

"It absolutely *does* have something to do with me! Let the Golden Duo be reborn!"

Enta had been waiting to hear those exact words, so he didn't hesitate. "Okay, Kazuki, I'm passing the ball!" He aimed and sent the ball soaring high up through the air.

Kappa-Kazuki leaped up with it, performing an overhead kick. "Enta! Here it is, straight to your heart! Miracle ☆ Shoot!" In the next instant, Kazuki's powerful kick sent the ball whizzing through the air like a bullet, slamming straight into Enta's stomach.

"Guuuuh...!"

The ball's trajectory remained unchanged as it soared onward, sinking into the net of the goalpost. Toi, acting as the goalkeeper, wrinkled his face in frustration.

"Nice shot!!" Even as he spat blood, Kappa-Enta savored his moment of happiness. But... *Ah, no way. There's just no way. This delusion is just too much.*

With an effort, Enta brought himself back to reality—just as the real Kappa-Kazuki called over to him.

"Hey, Enta!"

"Okay, this is my chance to casually... Kazuki, here, pass!" Enta sent the ball flying forward with a smack, but Kazuki only stood there and let it roll uselessly past him.

"Sorry, I actually have to use the bathroom."

The ball rebounded off the wall and slowly rolled back toward Enta, whose shoulders sank in disappointment. "I should've known it was hopeless."

As he stared at the locked door to the bathroom, a voice called out from behind him. "Staying in this form isn't going to do him any good," said Toi.

Enta's temper flared. "Like I need you to tell me that!"

Next, the three of them ventured to Sumida Park.

"There's a perfect cucumber patch just ahead!" said Enta. "You love cucumbers, right, Kazuki?"

"Yeah!"

"What the heck is a 'cucumber patch' anyway...?" Kappa-Toi was certain there had to be some better excuse the other boy could've come up with.

Kazuki stopped dead in his tracks. Just up ahead was...

"Nyantaro! Come here!"

Haruka in his wheelchair, his father pushing him along from behind.

Domp, domp, domp, domp, domp...!

Kappa-Kazuki sped off into the distance, leaving the others in his dust.

"He ran..." Enta mumbled.

"I knew it."

"Ribbit."

PLATE 6

Haruka

SCENE 3

"**S**ORRY YOUR FOOD'S so late today, Nyantaro."

"Mreeow." Nyantaro chowed down greedily on the Fishtopia kibble, meowing back in response as if to say she didn't mind at all.

"Hey, Nyantaro, Kazu-chan will come home, right?"

The cat didn't have an answer for that. Nor did anyone else, for that matter.

Haruka pulled out his phone. Having finished her meal, the feline flopped over and began snoozing.

"I hope this reaches him," Haruka whispered in prayer as he pressed the send button. Static suddenly flew across his screen, and a crimson red heart appeared. "Huh? I don't remember downloading this app..."

A shadow was suddenly cast over Haruka. "And who is this naughty boy?"

He looked up to find a uniformed police officer in front of him. It was Reo, with his dark skin, sharply pointed teeth, and bold smile.

Haruka nervously asked, "A-am I in trouble?"

"Why would you think that?"

"Because I stole Kazu-chan's smile from him."

"Who is 'Kazu-chan'?" asked Reo.

"My older brother. He hasn't come home since yesterday," Haruka confided, looking down at the ribbon headdress in his lap.

"Yeah? You're just like me, then. My partner left me yesterday and hasn't come back either."

"Mr. Policeman, are you naughty too?"

Reo looked dumbfounded for a moment but soon smiled and dismissed the notion. "Hah, of course not! My partner's the naughty one. He keeps a cool face, but he continues to betray me again and again. Like a doll, empty of all emotion." Reo held in his hand a ningyo-yaki, a chilled sweet baked into the face of a doll.

"I just want my brother to smile..."

"Oh?"

Haruka could feel the other man's gaze on him. He turned to find Reo's eyes peeled wide open, staring over at him.

"In that case, show me. What lies behind your door? Desire? Or love?" Reo's large hand covered the boy's sight, and Haruka's eyelids slowly closed. "Only those who can connect to their desires have the ability to grasp the future in their hands."

Reo reached out his arms to cradle the slumbering boy, but Nyantaro leaped up, her fur standing on end as she hissed at Reo.

Reo spared her a brief glance and muttered, "Be gone."

"Mreeeeeeow...!"

The words alone were enough to send the cat hurtling through the air.

Reo faced no further interference after that. He pulled Haruka into his arms and disappeared from the riverside.

"Enough, just be honest with him already!"

"I said I don't want to!"

Kappa-Toi watched in exasperation as the other two repeated the same argument in an obnoxious, unending loop. Kazuki latched on to the side of a raised flowerbed at the riverside, trying to fend off Enta's attempts to peel him off. "Let go already! I don't want to see him, Haruka's better off without me!"

"You know, Haruka's always been worried about...gweh!" The loop ended abruptly when Nyantaro came crashing through the air. The cat landed squarely on top of Enta's head, then started frantically licking at her ruffled fur.

"Nyantaro!" exclaimed Kazuki. "What the...what happened?!"

Kappa-Kazuki was aghast when he returned to the promenade. His little brother had been sitting there moments before, but now he was gone, his wheelchair left behind, empty.

"Haruka's gone?!"

Their father was slumped over his table at the coffee shop on the terrace.

"Your dad's out cold!"

"Tch, who the heck would've...?" Kappa-Toi was quick on his feet as well, racing around to see if they could spot anyone suspicious in the area.

As Kazuki stood frozen, his phone pinged to alert him of a new message. He whipped it out from the pouch under his shell—a space which existed in a separate dimension, ensuring anything left there wouldn't be damaged by water—and looked at the screen in surprise.

"Rii-ii-ii-ing! Rii-ii-ii-ing!" The plate atop Keppi's head transformed into a rotary phone and began obnoxiously mimicking the sound of an incoming call.

"Ugh, that's just creepy," commented Kappa-Enta.

"What the heck are you doing?!"

As Enta and Toi watched, Keppi lifted the receiver from the top of his head and answered. "Yes, good afternoon, ribbit. Yes... all right...very well, ribbit."

The receiver gave an audible clang as he returned it to the hook. Then Keppi reported, "I've got information coming in from a reliable source, ribbit. Yasaka Haruka has been kidnapped by the imperial army, ribbit."

"Seriously? The imperial army?! Wait, who are they?" Kappa-Enta asked, confused by the unfamiliar name.

"An army from the Empire that destroyed the Kappa Kingdom. Our enemies, ribbit."

"And what will they do with him?" Toi asked, wanting Keppi to get to the point.

"...Kill him and turn him into a Kappa Zombie, ribbit."

Enta and Toi sucked in surprised breaths when they heard that, but another voice cut in: "I won't let them!"

They glanced back at Kappa-Kazuki, who looked like an entirely different kappa now. A light burned in his eyes that hadn't been there before. "I will save Haruka!"

Sarazanmai

PLATE 6

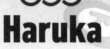

Haruka

SCENE 4

BY THE TIME Reo returned to the police box, Mabu was back from his maintenance run.

"Reo, where were you? And that child... We were told not to act alone."

"Hmph! Like I need to hear that from you." Reo didn't even try to hide his irritation toward his partner as he placed Haruka on a folding metal chair. The boy was still lost deep in sleep. "Now, let us open a door..."

Mabu didn't challenge him any further as Reo aimed his gun, just like he always did. "Is it desire?"

"Or love?"

A large taiko drum appeared above Haruka's head.

"Desire Extraction!"

"The Otter Empire?!" Kappa-Enta's cry of dismay echoed along the evening riverside. Kazuki and his kappa comrades were at an area beside the Sumida River encircled by a crescent-shaped railing and overgrown with shrubs.

"The war between us kappa and the otters has stretched on for many years, ribbit. Now...please follow me, ribbit."

Ploop!

Keppi leaped into the pool of water by the shrubs. Diving down to follow, the boys soon realized that the wall of the structure stretched on indefinitely. The plate on Keppi's head shone bright as he led the group, its light providing a dim illumination of the way ahead, though they still couldn't see the bottom at all.

"How did we get wrapped up in all of this?" Kappa-Toi asked, voicing a question that had been circling his brain.

"The thing we were struggling over was the Desire Energy from people's shirikodama, ribbit."

A faded mural appeared along the wall. The images were records of the past, depicting what had happened between the kappa and otters.

"After the Otter Empire drained all of the Desire Energy from the Kappa Kingdom, it set its eyes on the human world, ribbit."

"So, you're a survivor of the Kingdom, then..." Toi realized.

At some point along their journey, the vertical channel shifted into a horizontal one, and they were able to break the surface once more. The only thing they could see in the darkness of the tunnel was the steady glow of Keppi's head plate.

"I'm the only one capable of producing Wishing Plates, ribbit. If the Empire knew about me, they would be after my life, ribbit."

They could see the light of an exit in the distance. Once they swam past it, they found themselves inside an enormous structure.

Unfortunately, their momentum came to a screeching halt as they went tumbling down a seemingly endless waterfall.

"Waaaaaaaaaah?!"

The place's white framework expanded around them. When they looked deeper within, they could see a countless number of boxes being transported across the space, almost as if this were an enormous warehouse for a distribution company.

"What in the world is this place?" Kappa-Kazuki asked in disbelief.

As they continued plunging through the air together, Keppi replied, "This is the Otter Empire's secret base, ribbit!"

Tentacles stretched out from his body, wrapping around Kazuki and the others. In the next instant, Keppi transformed himself into a parachute and began smoothly gliding through the air.

"Where is Haruka?!"

"They put everything into boxes, ribbit."

"So, we have to open all these boxes and check?!" Enta gasped.

"Like we've got the time for that!" said Toi.

"What did you say?!"

Kazuki ignored his two comrades as they began to bicker—now, of all times—and started to think. "Maybe..." He pulled out his phone from his shell and dialed a number.

Brrrrrring... Brrrrrring...

Enta and Toi both gulped as they watched.

"Please, ring...!"

Suddenly they heard the faint sound of an incoming call coming from somewhere.

Brrrrring... Brrrrring...

Where? Which box?

There, amid the countless boxes carried along on conveyor belts, Kazuki spotted one with a heart and the kanji for spring written on it—"Haru!"

"I found him! He's in that box! Huh?!"

Just when he'd finally found his little brother's box, it plummeted off the end of the conveyor belt and landed on a pallet of other boxes. An enormous red crane clamped onto the pallet and began to carry the whole pile of them away.

"Haruka!" Kappa-Kazuki and the others raced after the crane. They slid down along the framework of the structure before darting down narrow pathways. Unfortunately, the crane only seemed to get farther away.

"Ack! Stop!" Kazuki had been leading the others when he suddenly slammed to a stop. When the others peered out from behind him, they realized the path abruptly ended. "What do we do now?"

Kazuki felt himself losing all hope, but Enta just snatched him up by the scruff of his neck and flung him through the air as hard as he could. "Hmph!"

"Gah!"

Kappa-Kazuki landed with a thunk on the metal plank on the other side of the gap.

"Hyaaaah!"

"Guh!"

Soon, Toi also came hurtling through the air after him. Kazuki sprang to his feet and shouted back after his friend, "Enta!"

Enta heaved Keppi through the air and shouted, "Go, Kazuki! Don't give up on Haruka!"

Time was of the essence right now. Kazuki and the others decided to hurry on ahead without their comrade.

A light suddenly began flashing red as a siren blared. They could see a barred gate ahead of them, beginning to slide itself shut.

"The gate!"

"No!"

Kappa-Toi leapt and smoothly slid forward, ducking under the gate. *Gah-gon!* It creaked in resistance as it hit his shell, propping it up just enough for Kazuki and Keppi to squeeze past.

"Kuji!"

An instant later, a durable fence slammed down between them, locking Toi out. He gave Kazuki a bitter smile as he said, "Jinnai and I will catch up, I swear."

Kazuki and Keppi found themselves on an elevator that gradually began to descend.

"You can still get him back," Toi called after them. "So keep running!"

As he waited for the elevator to come to a stop, Kazuki chewed his friends' words over in his head. He couldn't let their sacrifices go to waste.

Ga-thunk. As the elevator came to a stop, the two snuck out the doors. Before them loomed a hulking cylindrical structure spanned by an enormous bridge. The crane came soaring down from above them, its claws locked onto the pallet that contained Haruka's box. It came to a stop just in the middle, by the very tip of the bridge that extended inward. Black flames began bursting out of the taiko-shaped engines surrounding the center, almost like some sacred ritual.

Kazuki started over the bridge, sprinting toward the middle. There wasn't much distance left between him and the crane now. "Haruka, just a bit more...!"

Just then—

Ka-klink!

He heard the cold sound of metal as the crane's arms sprang open. The solid pallet of boxes came apart as they were sent sprinkling through the air. The sight before him seemed to play out in slow motion as Haruka's box went plummeting down into that valley of darkness.

"Haruka! Harukaaaaaaaa!" The sound of his shrieking was swallowed up by the gaping emptiness in front of him.

Bom, bom, bom... The blaze from the engines gradually began to fade. It was almost like watching the flame of someone's life being snuffed out.

Kappa-Kazuki was crumpled to the ground in a daze. On the opposite side of the pathway, Toi and Enta arrived, though they were frozen in place by what they just witnessed.

"No way, it can't be..."

"No!"

Kazuki was white as a sheet by the time he heard a voice call out from behind him. "Do you want to save Yasaka Haruka, ribbit?"

He glanced back to find Keppi. "*Can* I save him?"

"I can transfer your shirikodama to him, ribbit. If I do that, his life will be restored."

"You mean it?"

"There's no other way, ribbit."

Before Kazuki could say anything, Kappa-Toi shouted from the other side of the chasm. "Wait! If he loses his shirikodama, what happens to him? Will he die like the Kappa Zombies?!"

That immediately made Enta bristle in refusal. "You can't do that! Absolutely not!"

Keppi leaped over to stand on the tip of the crane as he continued, "Humans are connected by their shirikodama, ribbit. If you lose it, you won't be able to connect with people anymore. This world is linked together in one great circle, and you'll be flung outside of it."

Kazuki echoed the words to himself. "Flung outside the circle..."

"Indeed. With your shirikodama removed, it will be as if Yasaka Kazuki never existed in this world at all, ribbit. All memories involving you—events, objects, everything—will cease to exist, ribbit."

"What the heck? That's worse than dying!" Kappa-Enta roared, disturbed by the thought.

"So, the Kappa Zombies we defeated, it was like they never existed at all?" Toi realized.

"You can't do that, Kazuki!"

Kappa-Kazuki didn't respond to Enta's cries. Instead, he aimed a question at Keppi. "Does that mean...Haruka's accident would have never happened?" His mind flashed back to that day.

"...Indeed, ribbit."

As he looked down at the ground, a thin smile suddenly appeared on Kazuki's face. "Okay. All right, then." He dragged himself up off the ground, resolved. "I'd like you to give my shirikodama to Haruka, then."

His voice was quiet, but it still carried through the open air all the way to Enta and Toi.

"All right, ribbit. Then jump down into this chasm, ribbit." Keppi pressed a button, transforming the crane into a giant hoist instead. "I'll take your shirikodama into my body for safekeeping, ribbit. We'll need to cut all your connections to people before I make the transfer, ribbit."

"Okay."

"Kazuki! Stop this!" Kappa-Enta shrieked at them.

"Stay right there!" Toi joined his shouts of protest, and the two went scrambling down the pathway.

Kazuki slowly stretched out his hand to grasp the chain dangling from the hoist. The chill of the steel against his skin seemed to clear away his thoughts. *I was never inside that circle to begin with,* he realized. *Everything will be perfect for them without me.*

He remembered what Haruka had told him: *From beginning to end, you and I are connected by a great big circle.* Kappa-Kazuki shook his head and stepped forward, resting his foot on the hook at the bottom of the chain.

This is my last chance...an opportunity for someone like me, who can't connect with others, to atone for what I've done.

Ba-chink!

He pressed the button to begin lowering the hoist. The chains rattled, echoing as the machine powered up and began to move.

"Stop it, Kazuki! Do you really think this would make Haruka happy?!" Enta bellowed as he ran.

"It's fine! Haruka will forget everything and move on. You, too, Enta. Soon you'll forget all about me."

"There's no way I could forget! Just stop already. No more! Kazukii!"

Toi sprinted along behind Enta, frantic. The hoist continued to plunge Kazuki farther down into the chasm. "Tch! We're not going to make it!" He skidded to a halt, having realized that they'd never catch up. Kazuki was gradually receding from them.

"Kazukiiiii!" Enta's cry echoed around them.

Baaaang! Baaaang! Light flashed as Toi whipped out a gun and fired it, smoke rising from the barrel. His bullets arced down into the hoist, hitting it in just the right spot to cause the machine to backfire.

Ga-rarararara...

The recoil sent the chain that had been lowering Kazuki into the abyss instantly skyrocketing upward.

"Wh-whoooaaa?!" Kappa-Kazuki's body flew up over the hoist. He danced through the air before landing with a *splat* in front of Enta.

"Kazuki!"

"You okay?!"

Kazuki remained splayed out on the ground, motionless, so the two each took one of his hands in theirs and heaved him back onto his feet. Now he was upright at least, and still safely breathing.

"Give us a break," said Toi.

Kazuki quietly muttered to his two relieved friends, "Why?" His face crumpled in frustration. "Why did you stop me?! I'm the one who wanted this, so keep out of it! It's better if I just don't exist—"

Thwack!

Kazuki's sentence hung in the air, unfinished, as heat blossomed on his cheek. He collapsed backward from the force of the blow.

Toi had socked Kazuki in the face. His fist was still clenched as he bellowed at his friend, "If you've got the time to run your mouth with that nauseating rubbish, then you've got time to use your brain and think of another way!"

"That's right! I won't forgive you if you just disappear on me like that!" Enta flared in agreement, leaping on top of his fallen friend's stomach. As Kazuki groaned in protest, he saw a blue string twirling above his eyes. Enta was dangling the old friendship bracelet above his head—the same one he threw out.

"Huh? I thought I threw that away."

"Haruka entrusted me with it, because he still hasn't given up! He believes in you and is waiting for you!"

"Haruka..." Kappa-Kazuki's trembling fingertips brushed over the bracelet.

"Verdict: Love. Box: Returned," announced a robotic voice, echoing around them.

Keppi, still balancing atop the crane, peered down into the chasm and noticed something. "Oh? He's still alive, ribbit."

A crane rose up from the abyss, carrying a single, tiny package. "That's Haruka's box!"

The machine began carrying the box through the air, shuttling it away from them.

"Harukaaaa!"

This time he *had* to get his brother back. Kazuki swore to himself as he and the others dashed after the box. As the crane disappeared in the distance, their group ran up on three large ducts, with Kazuki at the front of their line. They kept silent as they each hopped into a different duct.

Sarazanmai

PLATE 6

Haruka

SCENE 5

THE UNLIT DUCTS were slanted such that they just slipped along the sides on their way down. As he jetted through that darkness, unsure when it would end, Kazuki reflected back on the events of that afternoon.

When they first discovered that Haruka had been kidnapped, he'd received a message on his phone. One from his brother. It was the longest one he had ever received from Haruka before, and it began like this:

To Sara-chan,

This will be the last message I send to you.

Haruka had written it knowing full well that Kazuki would be the one reading it.

I enjoyed every single day that I was able to connect with you. So now that it's at an end, can I tell you a secret I haven't been able to share with anyone else?

The angle of the duct suddenly ended, planting him squarely on even ground with no light in sight. Kazuki rolled slightly as he landed but soon hopped to his feet, desperately throwing one leg in front of the other.

I did something really bad, you see. I really love my brother, but I hurt someone he really loves.

"No, Haruka, you've got it wrong!" Kappa-Kazuki choked out, speaking to his little brother even though his words would never reach him. He continued aimlessly sprinting forward. Meanwhile, as Haruka still lay fast asleep in his box, tears beaded at the corners of his closed eyes.

I chased after my brother back then because I was scared. Scared he was going to leave me behind. That day, I picked up something his real mother dropped.

It was the sakura fragrance bag. Haruka recognized the scent because he'd smelled it on Kazuki's clothes when he'd come home.

"Oh, could you be Haruka-kun?" the woman had asked him.

He'd been so much younger then, and he'd frantically yelled at her, "Don't take Kazu-chan from us! Go home! Don't come here again!"

She just smiled and said, "It's okay, don't worry." Her smile looked just like my brother's. And ever since then, Kazu-chan stopped smiling and even threw away his friendship bracelet. I know it's all my fault, but I just wanted him to stay with me, laugh with me.

Kazuki's legs got tangled up, sending him skidding to the ground.

I'm so happy for everything my brother's done for me.

He struggled back to his feet and started forward again, the friendship bracelet dancing around the base of his ankle as he moved.

That's why I'm not going to give up. I believe that Kazu-chan will come back and smile at me again!

A dim light shone in front of him.

"There's the exit!"

As he came sprinting out into the neighboring room, he found himself looking out over an enormous dump. When he glanced up, he saw the crane, Haruka's box dangling from it as it soared through the air toward the center of the room. It was headed for a line of those strange taiko drums floating overhead, fastened together to form a strange structure.

"There he is—Haruka!"

"Kazukii!"

He looked down, following the sound of Enta's voice. The other two boys had found their way here as well, though their exits led them to slightly different positions.

"We won't be able to reach him from here!" exclaimed Enta. "What should we do?!" He looked back at Toi, who was standing on a platform further down below.

Toi glared up at the drums and crane overhead and snapped, "Are we gonna have to go back and find another way?!"

Suddenly, the drums roared to life. In the middle of them were sharp, gleaming blades, giving off an eerie, clanking whir as they spun around. Toi spotted a sparkling pile of dust on the floor immediately below them.

"It's a shredder!"

They each felt a shiver run down their spines.

"Haruka's going to be ground to dust...!" Kappa-Kazuki gasped, any composure he still had now lost.

Enta glanced around the area. "There's gotta be something... Do you see anything?!"

"Anything? Like what?!" Kappa-Toi whipped his head around and spotted Keppi, who finally caught up to him.

After a brief moment of silence, Keppi suddenly transformed himself into a round ball. "Sometimes solutions require sacrifice, ribbit. I am sure it will pain you to have to do this, with how adorable and precious I am, but please throw—"

Gonk!

"—me?!"

Kappa-Toi slammed his foot down on the Keppi-ball. Then he bounced the ball up into the air, promptly slamming a kick into it, which sent it rocketing upward. "Jinnai, catch!"

Keppi groaned as he flew through the air. "Geeeugh!"

"Whoa!" The pass connected perfectly as Enta caught the sphere square in his hands.

"Now pass it up to Yasaka! Have him use that ball to stop the crane!"

Enta hesitated. "But Kazuki won't..."

"Enta!" a voice called from above. When he lifted his head, he saw Kazuki gazing down at him, his expression solemn. "Enta, please pass me the ball!"

"Okay, Kazuki, I'm leaving this one to you!" His deepest wish—the Golden Duo pass—was finally coming true. "Here you...gooooo!"

"Owwwww!"

The Keppi-ball went hurtling through the air straight toward Kazuki.

The crane carrying Haruka's box finally came to a stop just above the shredder.

Kazu-chan's a bit stubborn, but he's also straightforward— always heading straight toward the goal.

"Great job, Enta!" Kazuki got himself a running start before leaping into the air.

Ka-chink! The crane's arms opened, sending the box plummeting downward. Toi and Enta kept their eyes on Kazuki, praying.

He can be difficult to read, but he's very kind and warm. I know that well.

"Haruka, I'm never going to give up on you again!" His overhead kick landed hard on the ball, blasting it through the air.

His aim proved to be perfect, and the ball slammed right into Haruka's box. The recoil, however, sent Haruka's body tumbling out of the box and straight down toward the jaws of the shredder.

"Ribbit!"

A roar tore through the air as the blades ripped into the box. Its remnants crumbled to the floor in front of Toi, landing neatly on the pile that was already there. Haruka and Keppi were nowhere to be seen.

"Haruka!" Kappa-Kazuki called out weakly, praying as he stared into the air.

From out of the shadow of the shredder, Keppi appeared in parachute form, gliding gently downward. Haruka, still fast asleep, was cradled safely in his long arms.

I'm not the only one who wants to see Kazu-chan's smile, either.

"Haruka!"

He's at the center of a great big circle.

Kazuki caught his unconscious brother safely in his arms. Kazuki almost couldn't believe he was real; but the weight of Haruka's body and the heat of his skin were proof that he was really here, that Kazuki had regained something precious. Joy rippled up through his body.

"We did it!" the three called out gleefully, their voices rising through that large dumpsite with the word "Love" written over it.

"Sarazanmai!"

That night, the three of them went to the Desire Field that hung over the Azuma Bridge. There, they performed their best "sarazanmai" yet.

"Dishing it out!"

Until now, the three of them had always moved slightly disjointedly, but now they were perfectly in sync. They didn't hesitate when transferring the shirikodama to each other. None of them cared if their secrets leaked. There was something between them that couldn't be seen, couldn't be touched or verified in any way. Something ambiguous. But it was definitely there, linking them together—something shared between their entwined consciousnesses.

PLATE 6

Haruka

SCENE 6

"**T**HIS FEELS so much better!"

"Agreed."

Back at the Kappa Plaza, Enta and Toi had returned to their human forms and were speaking to each other normally.

"I don't know how to put this, but, um..." Enta started. "Sorry."

"Nah. It didn't bother me." Toi looked away as he answered.

Having finally learned to trust each other, the two turned their gaze to the third member of their group. Kazuki stood with his back to them. He'd been quiet since they regained their human forms, patting his hands over his body as if to confirm he'd really changed back.

"Would you have rather stayed a kappa, ribbit?" asked Keppi, who was badly battered after being kicked around repeatedly.

Kazuki touched the skin of his face as he replied, "It feels weird. I know I'm the same person I was yesterday, but it feels like I'm a whole new human being."

Enta and Toi watched quietly.

"But...this is really me," he said, finally looking back at them.

"Kazuki..."

"Hmph. "

Kazuki gave them a goofy, clumsy smile, as if his muscles were making this expression for the first time. Then he said something that he'd never said before: "Thank you. I'm glad the two of you are with me!"

Reo and Mabu

REO AND MABU had their backs pressed against one another, floating atop an enormous drum submerged in water.

"The target you captured was stolen from us, and now they know our location," said Mabu. "Your carelessness has hindered our mission, Reo."

"Don't get so angry! What that kid had was love, anyway. We don't have any use for that. Ha. Ha ha... Bwa ha ha!"

"Reo, what's wrong?"

"That boy did us a favor! We've hit the jackpot!"

A giant monitor in the background revealed an image of Keppi flying in to Haruka's rescue.

"At last, I've found it. Hope for us!"

Sarazanmai

Lost Desire
and the Beginning of an Endless Night

IT WAS YEAR 333 of the Kappa Kingdom. The prolonged, drawn-out conflict with the Otter Empire was finally coming to an end. In the past, the river between the two countries seemed impassable, but they found a way to cross it—launching a full-on assault against the Kappa Kingdom in the process.

The crown prince, Keppi, was in his royal quarters, writhing in agony. Dark desires swelled within him, threatening at any moment to tear him apart.

The sliding door into the prince's spacious quarters was suddenly thrust open. Two figures appeared: Reo and Mabu, decked out in black military uniforms. "We found you!"

But just as Reo stepped forward, something happened.

"My desire...is going to spliiiit!" Something sinister suddenly emerged from Prince Keppi's body. "D-d-d-d-darkness!"

"Reo! Watch out!"

The blast ripped through the quarters, and the structure running the Kappa Kingdom crumbled.

An injured Reo squatted down amid the rubble, cradling a dying Mabu in his arms. "Why...why would you step in front of me?"

Mabu grasped Reo's trembling hand firmly and said, "Don't let go of your desires. Only those...who can connect to their desires... have the ability to...grasp the future in their hands..." Suddenly, Mabu's hand went limp.

"Mabuuuuuu!"

All around them, flames swallowed up the ruined Kappa Kingdom, dyeing the sky above them crimson.

No one could have predicted the path that lay ahead of the two. It seemed like nothing but endless, pitch-black despair stretched before them.